Cypress Lake

By

Graysen Morgen

2014

Cypress Lake © 2014 Graysen Morgen
Triplicity Publishing, LLC

ISBN-13: 978-0988619685
ISBN-10: 0988619687

Printed in the United States of America
First Edition – 2014
Cover Design: Triplicity Publishing, LLC
Interior Design: Triplicity Publishing, LLC

Also by Graysen Morgen

Special thanks to CJ, my eagle eyes down under for catching my mistakes and never being afraid to give it to me straight. *Tu mi tieni sulle mie dita dei piedi, amico.*

I dedicate this book to the woman who is my partner in life, my wife in marriage, and the mother of my child. Without her, none of what I do every day would be possible. *Ti amo e vorrei andare fino agli estremi confini della Terra per proteggere voi.*

Prologue

Cypress Lake was a small town, surrounding a large lake spanning five miles long and two miles wide, with a population of a little over one thousand. The overnight 911 operator received a break-in call just after three a.m. for one of the rented lakeside houses. She put the call into the computer and radioed one of the two sheriff's deputies on duty.

Deputy Vince Wagner arrived at the two-story house five minutes later with the lights flashing on his patrol car. He got out of the car, shining his flashlight at all the windows as he stepped onto the walkway.

"Cypress Lake Sheriff's Office," he said, pulling the screen door back and knocking loudly.

A woman opened the front door. She was dressed in a bathrobe, and her hair was pulled haphazardly up in a clip, with strands hanging down here and there. She looked at the young red-haired man standing on the other side of the screen.

"Did you call about a break-in?" he asked.

"Yes. Someone was trying to get into the back of the house. I think your lights scared them off," she replied shakily.

"I'm going to walk around and take a look."

He moved around the side of the house to the patio, his flashlight casting a soft glow over the back of the house and across the yard. Satisfied that the intruder hadn't left any evidence behind, he walked back to the front door, knocking again.

"I don't see anything, except a few scratches on the door jam. These rented lake houses are broken into often, but it's usually when they're in between renters. Whoever it was, probably thought the place was vacant," he informed her.

"I've been here for a couple of weeks," she replied, pulling her robe tighter around her naked body.

"Make sure all your windows are closed and locked, and you might want to call the owner about putting deadbolts on the doors. He probably won't come back but call us if he does."

Chapter 1

Chief Deputy Dani Ricketts' computer chimed, signaling a new call had come in. She ignored the readout on the screen and was about to pull into the parking lot of Papa's Smokehouse to feed her growling stomach when her radio crackled.

"What's your twenty?" the man in dispatch asked.

Dani pulled her white Chevy Trailblazer with Cypress Lake Sheriff's Office written on the side in green, yellow and silver, into a parking space. She grabbed the microphone attached to the side of the computer.

"Papa's. Do you want me to bring you something?" she answered, clicking the button at the bottom of the screen to bring up the open call list.

The bold red letters at the top of the page for the call that she'd ignored grabbed her attention. She immediately threw the truck into drive, flipped the switch for the lights and siren, and stomped the gas pedal, peeling out onto the two-lane road.

"We have a report of a body in the water out on Lake Drive," dispatch radioed.

"Copy. I'm 10-86. ETA five minutes. Who's on scene?" Dani asked, speeding through town.

A dead body was high priority in Cypress Lake. They were a small town with a small population, and although they had their fair share of minor offenses, they rarely had any major crime. It had been a couple of years since they'd had a potential homicide and Dani's heartbeat raced a little with excitement, however she had a feeling this was

3

probably another drowning. Those types of calls happened occasionally, mostly because the town's residents surrounded the large lake. Each year a few of their older residents had heart attacks while swimming and subsequently drowned.

"Deputy Nyman just arrived."

"Okay, you'd better inform the sheriff. I know he's in a meeting with Mayor Olsen, but this is priority."

Dani switched her radio to the secure channel that was designated for high-profile calls. She knew the deputy would've immediately changed his radio to that channel once he'd arrived on scene. In a small town, many people had police scanners and radios and if the sheriff's office and fire department didn't use specific channels for special calls, the entire town would show up at the scene.

"Wilbur, I'm two minutes out. Tape off the area and don't let anyone near the scene," she radioed to him.

"Yes, ma'am," the part-time deputy answered shakily. This was the first time he'd ever seen a dead body.

"Start gathering statements," she said, checking the house number as she turned onto Lake Drive. She nearly ran off the road when she saw the number 321. That was a house she had been very familiar with growing up. She hadn't been there since the family who owned it moved away over twelve years ago. It had been rented out to various people ever since.

*

The tires on Dani's SUV crunched the gravel as she pulled into the driveway behind a small blue car. The deputy's matching truck was parked on the side of the road slightly in the grass, which was protocol when arriving on a scene.

Dani threw the truck into park and typed a note on the computer to dispatch that she'd arrived on scene before getting out. She reached for the radio microphone attached to her uniform above her right shoulder.

"Wilbur, what's your twenty? I'm on scene," she radioed.

"Backyard," he replied.

Dani looked up at the off-white, two-story house. It was about the same size as most of the other three-bedroom, two-bathroom lake houses. She'd spent most of her childhood running up and down the stairs inside, building sandcastles in the small beach area near the shallow water, and jumping off the end of the dock. She shook her head, forcing the memories to fade away as she walked around the side of the house.

The deputy down by the dock saw her round the corner and headed in her direction as fast as he could walk. He was dressed in a sheriff's uniform similar to hers, but his star shaped badge was black, indicating that he was only a part-time deputy. Dani liked him. He had a lot of potential and she'd gone to bat for him recently when the sheriff had wanted to cut him from the part-time roster. So far, he hadn't let her down.

"What do we have?" she asked.

"The body's floating face down, but it appears to be male," he said.

Dani walked with him across the small yard and onto the old wooden dock. The body had washed up against the dock and was wedged in the rocks. Dani squatted down on the edge, careful not to fall in as she peered over the side. The deceased person had short brown hair and was wearing jeans and a blue and black flannel shirt. She took a few pictures with the camera on her cell phone since it took clearer, higher resolution pictures than the cheap camera that had been issued to her.

"Did you call for Dr. Harper?" she asked.

"No. I was waiting for you."

Dani nodded, taking the notepad out of her pocket and making a few notes. "What about the renter? Did you speak to him?"

"She's the one who found the floater. She said she stepped out onto the second-floor balcony from the master bedroom and saw something in the water. She ran down the stairs and outside, but once she saw what it was, she knew it was too late to save the person."

"Hmm … alright. You told her not to leave, right?"

"Yes."

Dani grabbed her cell phone from her pocket and called Dr. Henry Harper. He was the director of the local hospital, which was more like a glorified clinic. He was also a pathologist and doubled as the town medical examiner when they had a suspicious death or needed an autopsy.

"We need to get it out of the water," she said, looking back at him. The expression on his face made her laugh. "Okay, I guess *I* need to get it out of the water," she chuckled, shaking her head. "Unfold the body bag and lay it out in the grass. I'll go in and pull it up on the sandy embankment over there. You're going to have to help me haul it up and get it in the bag though, so if you need to barf you had better do it now."

"I'm fine," he said, turning slightly green as he followed her off the dock.

Dani walked back up to her truck to retrieve a pair of rubber gloves and put on her waders. She returned quickly, wearing the waist high rubber pants, and stepped into the cold water. Spring was only a couple of weeks away, and even though the warm sunny days had begun to arrive, the lake water wouldn't begin to warm up for another month. She walked through the knee-deep, crystal-clear water, careful not to fall as she stepped across the sandy bottom and over the river rocks scattered about. Reaching the body, she grabbed the leg nearest to her and pulled the carcass away from the large rocks near the dock. The body began to sink once it was freed. Dani quickly grabbed the corpse's arm with her other hand, dragging it towards the shore.

Wilbur moved down to the shoreline and helped her haul the body up out of the water. Dani rolled it over, gasping when she saw the large gash across the pale, blotchy flesh of the man's neck. His face had been slightly chewed off on one side, more than likely by fish that inhabited the water. Wilbur stumbled backwards, falling down in the sand on the embankment.

"Someone cut this man's throat," Dani said nervously, examining him a little closer and taking more pictures with her phone's camera. "He hasn't been in the water long, a few days maybe. Are you okay?" she asked, looking up at the wide-eyed deputy who was wiping his mouth on the back of his hand. She was glad she hadn't had lunch, otherwise she'd be puking next to him.

"Yeah, yeah. I just wasn't expecting that."

"What have we got?" a squeaky male voice echoed across the open yard.

Dani turned to see the doctor walking towards her, pushing a stretcher.

"Hey, Henry. Looks like a homicide," she answered.

"Whoa, that's an understatement," he said, walking closer and squatting down. "He's not bloated."

"Yeah, I noticed that too," Dani agreed.

"Let's get him loaded up. I'll have a preliminary report for you tomorrow probably."

They worked together to stuff the dead body into the black bag and load it onto the stretcher and then she pulled her waders off.

Dani grabbed the radio microphone clipped to her shoulder. "Dispatch, send another deputy to Lake Drive and alert the sheriff. We have a 10-35."

"Roger," the dispatch operator replied.

"Let's go walk the dock and see if we can gather any evidence. This property just turned into a major crime scene," Dani said, walking back down the dock.

Ten minutes later, another deputy arrived and met them in the backyard.

"I was just here a week or two ago for a 10-14," Vince said, walking up to Dani.

"What do you mean?" she asked, raising an eyebrow.

"Someone was trying to break in the back door," he replied. "What happened?"

"We found a man in the water by the dock with his throat cut," Wilbur exclaimed.

"I heard about that call. Are you sure this was the house?" Dani asked.

"Yeah, it was around three in the morning. I remember because the renter was a little ruffled, but very easy on the eyes. I've never seen her before."

"Alright, I'll pull the report. I've already walked the dock and the yard, but you two take another pass. We're looking for blood, torn clothing, drag marks, anything out of the ordinary. Wilbur, what's the name of the renter? It's time I go have a word with her."

Wilbur pulled the small notebook from his pocket and flipped a few pages. "Kristen Malone," he replied.

Dani's breath caught in her throat, causing her to cough slightly. "That's not her name. The Malone family owns this house. She must have given you the owner's name."

"Well, that's what the renter said her name was. Kristen Malone," he corrected.

Dani's head jerked as if she'd been slapped. "What?" Her lungs deflated and she felt her stomach dry heave.

"Is something wrong?" Wilbur asked.

"No. I ... I didn't realize she was back in town. She's not a renter. She's the owner," Dani said as she turned around and began walking towards the house. She had thought about the day she would finally see Kristen again and after twelve years she still had no idea what she was going to say to the woman who had broken her heart. Her blood boiled and her heart raced. The closer she got to the front door, the angrier she got. *Damn you, Kristen.*

Chapter 2

Kristen had stayed away from the windows, choosing to hide out in her old bedroom on her laptop as the sheriff's deputies traipsed around her backyard. Seeing the dead body floating by the dock had thrown her mind into a whirlwind.

Loud knocking on the front door startled Kristen. She took the stairs two at a time and pulled the door open swiftly. She noticed the shape of a woman standing on the other side of the screen door. Kristen pushed the screen out wide, taking in the woman in front of her. The sheriff's deputy had dark brown hair pulled back in a short ponytail and black sunglasses with black lenses. She wore the same button-down khaki shirt over a white undershirt and dark green trousers with a utility belt that housed a gun, a radio, and handcuffs as the other deputy who arrived earlier, but her uniform fit her athletic frame nicely.

"Officer …" Kristen said, trying to make out the last name stitched on the brown patch above the woman's right breast. "Ricketts?" she gasped, recognizing the name.

Dani stared at the woman in front of her in disbelief. She had light brown hair with natural highlights that hung just below her shoulders in lazy waves, big chocolate brown eyes, and suntanned skin. The red t-shirt and jeans she wore hugged her slender figure perfectly, enhancing her average sized breasts and trim waist. Dani watched as she ran her hand through her hair, pushing it back over her shoulder and revealing small gold hoop earrings. The young girl she remembered from high school had grown into a beautiful woman.

"It's deputy. Chief deputy to be exact," Dani growled.

Kristen stepped over the threshold with a puzzled look on her face. "Dani?"

Dani backed up a step, pushing her sunglasses up on her head, revealing her gorgeous green eyes. "How long have you been back?" she asked.

"I ..." Kristen knew she might run into Dani Ricketts while she was home, but she'd hoped she could do what she needed to do and get out of town without seeing the one person who could bring her to her knees with a simple look. She appeared visibly stunned when Dani's eyes met hers.

"Kristen?" Dani huffed as her eyebrow arched.

"What are you doing in a sheriff's uniform?"

"I'm the one asking the questions. You've been gone for a long time, people change. They grow up, get jobs, and move on. Now, how long have you been in town, and why the hell is there a dead body in your backyard?" Dani snapped.

"Don't yell at me. I have no idea! I stepped onto the balcony to eat my lunch and saw something in the water. I haven't even been down on the dock since I got here."

"And when was that?"

"Tomorrow will be three weeks."

"Why are you back?"

"I own the house now and I'm selling it."

Dani leaned back, looking towards the road. "I don't see a *for sale* sign."

"I'm packing up my family's stuff first."

Dani nodded, turning back towards her.

11

"One of my deputies chased a prowler away recently, is that correct?" she asked, making notes on the small pad that she carried in her pocket.

"Yes." Kristen ran a flustered hand through her hair, pushing it back off her shoulder again.

"Do you have any idea who it was?"

"No. He told me the rented houses get broken into a lot this time of year, usually when they're between renters."

"What about the guy in the water? Any idea who he is?"

"No. I didn't see his face. I realized it was a dead body, and I screamed and ran inside to call 911."

Dani pulled her phone from her pocket and scrolled to the close-up picture of the man's face. "Do you recognize him? Was this the prowler?"

Kristen peered at the picture and backed away in disgust. "No. I don't know if that was him or not. That's gross."

"It's a lot more than a dead body, Kristen. That guy's throat was cut, and he hadn't been in the water long." Dani scrolled to the next picture that exposed his sliced throat and showed it to Kristen.

"Oh my God, you don't think I did this … do you, Dani?"

"I have no idea! I don't see you or hear from you for twelve damn years, and I get called out here for a dead body that turns out to be a homicide, and you just happened to be back."

"Do I need to call my lawyer?"

"I don't know. You tell me," Dani countered.

"I can't believe you're standing on my doorstep harassing me like this."

Dani blew out a frustrated breath. Seeing Kristen again had thrown her off balance. She'd let the pieces of her broken heart resurface, leading her down an angry path, instead of thinking like an officer, or in this case, a detective. She slipped her sunglasses back on.

"Don't leave town. I'll be in touch," she said, turning around and walking towards the backyard.

*

Kristen watched her walk away before closing the door. The anger in Dani's voice was a surprise, but the pain in her deep green eyes had been unmistakable and had cut Kristen to the bone. She'd been shocked to see Dani in a uniform and the fact that she'd been slightly aroused when she'd first seen the deputy through the screen had made complete sense. Even after all the years between them, simply looking at Dani Ricketts still made her weak in the knees.

"I can't do this. I should've just followed my original plan and hired someone," she said, shaking her head as she pulled the curtain back, peering down at the three uniformed deputies gathered together on her dock. "Damn you, Dani. I've tried so hard to avoid seeing you. Who the hell knew you were a sheriff's deputy?"

She watched Dani pointing to the water and the dock before writing on the little notepad. She was obviously in charge of the two young men who nodded their heads, following her every move. *If you knew why I left you so long ago, you'd understand why I'm back, doing what I need to do to move on.*

*

13

Dani looked out across the water at the big green cypress trees that filled the wooded space between each of the houses that lined the lake. She watched the lake current flow past the end of the dock that she stood on. She was able to see through the clear, ten-foot-deep water, straight to the sandy bottom, littered with river rocks and water plants. Her nerves were still frazzled from seeing Kristen. She tried calming her racing pulse, but her mind was about as far from relaxed as it could possibly be.

"Do you think that woman in the house did this?" Wilbur asked.

"No," she replied. It was true. She didn't know Kristen Malone anymore, but the young girl she'd grown up with wasn't capable of physically harming anyone. Dani pursed her lips and blew out a deep breath. "The body was probably dumped from a boat and washed up into the rocks next to this dock. I think it's pure coincidence, but nothing is set in stone until we get the results from Henry and find out who he is."

"What do we do now?"

Dani looked at Vince and grinned. "Have you ever seen an autopsy?"

"No. Well, in the academy we had to watch one, but I stood in the back, so I didn't actually *see* it."

"Since I know he has a weak stomach ..." She smiled, nodding towards Wilbur. "You go ahead and catch up with Henry." She pointed to Vince. "See if he's started. I'm going to go meet with Sheriff Fisher and bring him up to speed. Wilbur, go back on patrol."

"Yes, ma'am." Wilbur smiled and headed towards his patrol car. He was happy to be reassigned. The dead body freaked him out.

"I'll check in with you in a little while," Dani said to Vince as she climbed into her SUV. She started the engine and backed out of the driveway.

Dani turned at the first road off Lake Drive, pulled into a parking lot and threw the truck into park as she bent her head down, pressing her forehead against the steering wheel. She hadn't been prepared for the rush of feelings that had come back to her when she'd seen Kristen. It was like the world had stood still during the brief, heated conversation that they'd shared.

"Why the hell are you back? More importantly, why the hell did you ever leave?" she said, shaking her head. "There are over two hundred houses around this lake and that damn corpse just had to wash up at hers." *I thought I had a better chance of being struck by lightning than ever seeing her again.*

Chapter 3

Dani walked into the sheriff's office, stretching her neck from side to side as she pushed her sunglasses up on her head. Her empty stomach was starting to make her feel queasy, but eating food was the last thing on her mind. She had no idea how long her day was going to be after finding the body out at Kristen's house and the only thing she really wanted was a cold beer.

"How bad is it?" Sheriff Fisher asked when Dani walked into his office, sitting down in the chair across from his old, dilapidated desk.

"It's a young male with his throat cut. Henry has him now, but from what I noticed on the scene, he wasn't bloated. That means he probably wasn't in the water long."

"What did the renter say? Do they have any idea who he is?"

"No and it's not a renter. Kristen Malone is back in town."

"Malone? I remember that name. The body was found at their dock?"

"The Malone family became residents here when I was only a few years old. I grew up with Kristen. Her family moved away towards the end of our senior year and their house has been a rental ever since. The body was washed up in the rocks against their dock on the south side of the lake."

"Hmm … do you think she has anything to do with this?" he asked, chewing on the corner of his thick white mustache.

"No. It would take someone awfully strong to cut a grown man's throat. She's an inch shorter than me and looks like she's in great shape, but I doubt she's strong enough to do something like that. I'll know more after Henry finishes his report. I sent Vince to observe the autopsy."

Sheriff Fisher laughed. "Poor kid."

"Wilbur lost his lunch at the scene, so I put him back on patrol. There's not much to do at this point anyway and he's only part-time."

"Make sure you check the missing person reports and cross check anything from the nearby cities that match his description. Let me know when you get that report. Mayor Olsen doesn't know about this yet and I want to make sure we have all our bases covered before I fill him in."

Dani nodded and went back to the makeshift closet she called an office. She emailed all the crime scene photos to herself, uploaded them onto her computer, and went to work checking the databases. She didn't have much to go on and the description of a 5'10", 160lb male with brown hair between the ages of 25 and 33 had over fifty hits on the larger database that covered the three nearby cities.

"Damn," she huffed. This was going to take the rest of the day and most of the night to weed through unless the medical examiner came up with something to positively ID the man.

A couple of hours later, Dani's stomach rumbled, reminding her dinner time was nearing and she'd had nothing to eat the entire day except for a glass of chocolate milk and a banana after her morning run. She reached into her side desk drawer and pulled out a cookie dough flavored protein bar. She tore open the wrapper, chewing nearly half the bar in one bite before the bitterly disgusting, sour taste coated her tongue. She tossed the rest of the bar into the trash can next to her and spewed the chewed-up pieces from her mouth.

"Yuck!" she spat as her stomach rolled. Her cell phone lit up and began vibrating on her desk. She answered it as she spit the last of the remnants into the can.

"Everything okay?" Henry asked.

Dani rolled her eyes, wishing desperately for a bottle of water to appear. "I'm fine," she replied. "Apparently, I need to check the dates on the food I leave lying around the station."

Henry laughed. "Your report's finished. I sent it over with Huckleberry Hound."

"What?" Dani snickered.

"That deputy you sent over had a hundred questions. He reminded me of that old blue dog cartoon. It's probably well before your time, kiddo."

"No, I know who you're talking about. I just don't picture Vince as Huckleberry Hound. He is a little inquisitive though. I figured he was a better choice than Wilbur, unless you wanted puke on your cadaver. He's a green as goose shit part-timer."

"No, I'd take the questions over the puking rookie any day. I need to get back to my live patients. Let me know if you have any questions about the report. I was able to get one solid fingerprint, so maybe you can ID him with that. His toxicology screen should be back in about two weeks, so I'll let you know as soon as I get it."

"Great. Thanks again, Henry." Dani hung up the phone and pulled the trash bag from the can, tying the top of it as she walked out of her office.

"Mine needs to go out too, if you're pulling maid duties," Sheriff Fisher called from his opened doorway.

"Does yours have rotten food in it too?" she grinned.

"Eww, Ricketts. I told you that health food was bad for you."

Dani rolled her eyes and walked through the back door of the station. She tossed the bag into the dumpster and turned around when she heard a siren in the distance. A minute later, Vince pulled into the parking lot, stopping and rolling his window down when he saw her.

"Tell me you didn't drive over here lit up because of an autopsy report." She raised an eyebrow, leaning down with her hands on the top of the door.

"I ... Uh, I thought this was urgent, so ..."

Dani shook her head. "We never run with lights and sirens unless it's an emergency. A simple report is NOT an emergency, Deputy Wagner." Dani stuck her hand into the car, grabbing the report folder from his hand. She checked the black digital watch on her left wrist. "Get back out on patrol. Your shift's almost over and there's nothing more to do on this case until tomorrow morning."

She stepped back as he drove away. Subsequently, her shift was ending soon too, but she still had another couple of hours to go before she'd be able to call it a day. She needed to get this man identified. Dani walked back into the building, stopping in the break room to grab a replacement bag for her trash can on the way to her office.

Back at her desk, she read through the report, page by page. Just as she had suspected, the deceased man had died from the wound on his throat. The wound on the right side of the neck was superficial and the jugular vein and carotid artery on the left side were both severed, indicating he had probably bled to death very quickly. He'd been in the water between forty-eight and seventy-two hours, but wasn't bloated, which meant he hadn't sunk to the bottom and resurfaced.

Dani wrote down a few points on the small pad from her pocket, noting his trachea hadn't been sliced through and the cut was more on the left side of the trachea and back to the ear, severing the arteries. Also, the beginning of the wound and sliced edges were inconclusive because of the various fish that had chewed on the opened flesh. So, it was uncertain as to which hand the killer may have used to hold the knife or what type of blade was used. She had just finished her notes when she heard her name followed by muffled cursing. She closed the file and stepped out of her office.

"Damn it. You owe me fifty cents! I wanted a diet soda, and the damn machine spit out a water!" Sheriff Fisher growled.

Dani laughed. "Well, you shouldn't make me refill it then. Besides, water is good for you."

"Just because you're one of those health nut freaks, doesn't mean the rest of us have to be too."

"There is nothing wrong with eating healthy and I hate to say it, but I'm not a health nut by any means. I can't stand the taste of kale, I eat meat, and ice cream and I have a long-standing relationship. I just try to eat healthily and drink lots of water. You should try it sometime," she replied, getting a water from the machine for herself.

"No, thanks. Do you remember when you tried to turn me into a gym rat? That didn't work either. So, get your damn water out of my diet soda slot on the machine or I'm promoting Vince to chief deputy."

Dani laughed, shaking her head as he started walking away, drinking the water. He knew where the key to the machine was located and could have easily traded the water for his precious soda, but he was too lazy to go through all the trouble. She knew he'd be pissed when he figured it out, but honestly the machine only had one slot for water and five slots for various sodas. She'd simply rectified the situation.

"Hey, I've finished reading Henry's report," she called to his back before taking a long swallow of the cold water.

He spun and walked back towards her as she ducked into her office. He sat down in front of her desk, still drinking his water. She grinned.

"Get on with it," he growled.

"There isn't much to go on. His arteries on the left side of his neck were severed, so he died within seconds and was already dead when he went into the water. He wasn't in the water long, two or three days at the most."

"You said he wasn't a floater, correct?"

"Yes. This leads me to believe he was dumped in that spot. I think if he'd been dumped further out in the lake he would've sunk instead of floating up to that particular dock and getting hung up in the rocks. Whoever did this wanted to make sure this man was dead, and their tracks were covered."

"That makes sense. What about the wound?"

"Fish pretty much destroyed the flesh, so it's impossible to tell which angle the blade traveled or even what type of blade was used. I did find something slightly interesting though. His throat was mainly only cut on the left side, and the trachea was barely cut at all. Most throat slices include severing the trachea."

"That sounds like a right-handed killer."

"I agree, but if he'd turned his head defensively, then it could easily be a left-handed killer. The results are inconclusive, so it could really go either way. There are no defensive wounds, but then again, a lot of the flesh on his hands was eaten away."

"Are you leaning towards the owner of the home?" Sheriff Fisher asked, tossing his empty bottle into her freshly lined waste basket.

"No. Although, this report makes me think whoever did this struggled a little bit, I don't think she could have held a man from behind that was four inches taller and thirty pounds heavier and cut his throat at the same time."

"Could you do it?" he asked.

"Me? I doubt it. I'm certainly strong enough to hold my own against a man of this guy's size, but to be able to hold him and cut his throat at the same time … no, no way. I'd have to be super woman. Besides, she doesn't have any defensive wounds. A grown man would be fighting like hell if someone was trying to cut his throat."

"I agree. So, what's your gut telling you?"

"Cutting someone's throat is way more physical than say shooting them. Either someone was trying to shut this guy up or send a message."

"Do we know who he is yet?"

"There's a print. I was just about to load it into our database when you went ape shit over the vending machine," Dani teased.

"Yeah, yeah. That situation better be straightened out before I come in tomorrow. Don't stay here all night. The good thing about a dead body is the fact that they don't have anywhere to go. He'll be on the same slab in the freezer in the morning."

"I know. I'm going to run this print and at least see if he's local before I head out for the night. I don't think there's a reason to alert everyone. At this point, he could be a drifter or caught up in some kind of drug deal gone wrong. If the word gets out, the entire town will be on edge."

"Exactly," he said. "That's why I'm waiting until we have a little more before I take it to Olsen. His beard's liable to turn purple when he finds out we have a murderer on the loose."

Dani waved goodbye as he passed by her open door on his way out. She had put the fingerprint into their computer system and was waiting for it to finish scrolling through their short list of offenders. Her mind drifted back to Kristen. Seeing her again was like pouring salt into an open wound. It stung deep down to her core, causing her anger to bubble to the surface. The one person she'd never wanted to see again had landed literally in her lap with a devilish smile spread across her face. Dani was tempted to drive back to the Malone house and have it out with Kristen once and for all. She probably didn't need to know the true reason behind the Malone Family's quick departure, but she wanted to know why Kristen chose to never return, not even for her.

She snatched her keys off the desk and jumped up out of her seat, functioning solely on adrenaline fueled by anger, but the beeping of the computer brought her attention back to reality. The program had finished running and the alert chime sounded because a match had been found. Dani sat back down and clicked on the results. The name *Paul Davis* was at the top of the page in bold letters with a small picture from his last arrest under it and his rap sheet below that. She and Kristen had gone to school with him. Dani knew he'd become an alcoholic and eventually became a bum, living in the woods. He'd dabbled in selling drugs here and there which was also listed on his record. She checked the latest resident report. Sure enough, his family still lived in Cypress Lake. She'd have to make an official visit to his parent's house in the morning to inform them of his death. This was the part of the job she didn't care for. She shook her head, turning the computer off.

Chapter 4

It was after eight p.m. when she climbed into her SUV and drove away from the station. She was tired and hungry enough to gnaw off her own arm. She lived closer to the middle of town in a tiny studio apartment above the Cypress Market, which was the mom-and-pop style general store her parents owned.

Dani parked in the back lot of the small building and took the metal stairs two at a time up to her apartment door. She walked inside the place she called home, which looked more like an extended stay type of hotel room than an actual apartment. She shed her utility belt, hanging it on one of the two chairs at the miniature dining table as a flash of orange streaked by, just about knocking her off her feet.

"Oh, come on. I'm not that late you asshole cat," she yelled. "Besides, there's still food in your bowl from this morning!" She shook her head and opened the door to the walk-in closet. It still amazed her that the five hundred square foot apartment had such a large closet, but it doubled as a storage area since there was no other storage space in the unit.

Dani changed into a pair of jeans, a tight black t-shirt that accentuated her athletic build, and sneakers. She pushed her ankle pistol into the back of her waistband, pulled the tail of her shirt down over it and slipped her wallet that concealed her badge into one back pocket and her cell phone into the other. Then, she pulled her hair free from the short ponytail it had been in for nearly thirteen hours and quickly brushed the dark brown strands that stopped at the top of her shoulders before tucking it behind her ear on the left side. She tossed a couple of cat treats on top of the food in the dish and grabbed her windbreaker from the coat rack by the door on her way out.

Dani crossed the street and walked briskly towards the hole in the wall pub called Muddy's, entering from the side door instead of the main entrance. The establishment was only a couple of blocks away and had been in the town for close to forty years.

"Evening, Chief," the bar owner grinned as she sat on a high-backed stool.

She smiled brightly, removing her jacket and laying it over the back of the stool.

"How's business, Ernie?" she asked as he pulled the white towel from his shoulder, wiping the bar in front of her. He popped the top on a bottle of light beer and slid it over to her. Dani took a long swallow.

"Oh, it's not too bad. The warmer weather's starting to bring people out. Can I get you something from the kitchen?" He pulled the pencil from behind his ear and waited to write her order on the pad in his hand.

Dani stared at the chalkboard behind him that listed the daily specials. "Turkey club and a bowl of vegetable soup."

"Coming up," he said.

One of the two TVs over the bar had the national news muted and the other had a college basketball game playing. She sipped her beer, deciding the game looked more appealing.

Ten minutes later, Ernie pushed an oval plate in front of her with her sandwich on one end and the bowl of soup on the other. He knew better than to offer the salt and pepper. She'd been coming into his pub a couple of nights a week for the better part of six years.

"Another beer?" he asked, sliding it down to her when she nodded.

A few of the town people sitting at the bar recognized her and said hello, but most of the time she was left alone, and she preferred it that way. The rented lake houses drew a lot of new faces to Cypress Lake for the winter months and then a completely different set for the summer. Occasionally, one of the new people in town would hit on her and she'd politely decline their offer. When she was in the mood, she'd accept the offer and spend the night with a beautiful woman with no strings attached, but that occasion was about as rare as finding a hundred-dollar bill in the street.

Dani alternated bites of the sandwich with spoonfuls of soup as she watched the game on the flat screen. She was three quarters of the way through her two-beer limit and contemplated ordering a shot after the day she'd had, but she changed her mind when she noticed the guy on the stool next to her working his way closer.

Great. She rolled her eyes.

"Can I buy you another?" he asked, eyeing her like a dog looking at a medium rare piece of steak.

She smiled brightly. "No, thank you. I'm afraid I've hit my limit for the night."

"Just one more. It's still early," he tried again.

She finished the last spoonful of soup in the bowl, smiling thinly and shaking her head no.

"How about a shot then?"

Dani had just about had enough of the eager man. She ignored him as she sipped the last of her beer.

"What's wrong? Your old man won't let you stay out?" he taunted.

The man on the other side of him laughed loudly.

"Maybe she doesn't like old farts," he countered.

Dani almost choked on her sandwich.

"Hey, fuck you, man. No one's talking to you," the guy next to her said.

"I don't blame her. I wouldn't talk to you either. Your breathe smells like a skunk's asshole," the other guy replied.

Dani set the sandwich down slowly, watching the two men in the reflection on the TV. The guy next to her jumped out of his seat, standing uneasily and lunging for the man next to him as the man tried to stand up on wobbly legs. Dani was out of her seat and between the two men with lightning speed.

"Break it up!" she shouted, slamming the guy that had been sitting next her, against the bar. The muscles in her arms flexed as she pushed the other guy back in the opposite direction. She pulled her wallet from her back pocket, flipping it open and displaying her badge. "I suggest you sit your asses down, unless you want to go to jail tonight," she yelled.

Both men put their hands up, shaking their heads no.

"Ernie, get these guys some coffee," she said, shaking her head and sitting back down.

"Holy shit," one of the guys huffed, getting back onto his stool.

"You two messed with the wrong girl," Ernie grinned.

Dani finished her sandwich and pushed the plate and bowl away. She pulled a twenty-dollar bill from her wallet, tossing it on the bar as she stood up.

"Call me if you hear any more out of these two tonight." She smiled, waving at Ernie as she exited through the side door.

She walked back to her apartment but climbed into her SUV instead of going up the stairs. She pulled out of the parking lot, fueled by temptation as she headed towards the lake. She turned onto Lake Drive, watching the houses go by until she came upon the one that was off limits. The back of the house was lit up and the same blue car from earlier in the day was parked in the driveway.

Dani fought the urge to stop as she slowed the truck to a crawl. Her mind was playing sinful pranks, making her remember making love to Kristen when they were barely old enough to drive cars. She would never stop wanting the woman inside of that house, but the anger bubbling at the surface deterred her thoughts. She pressed the gas and sped off.

They had been forced to go their separate ways and were now two totally different people. Their lives had intertwined overnight because of the homicide case and that case was Dani's top priority. She chided herself for even thinking about Kristen. Her heart had been torn to pieces twelve years ago and she wasn't about to let it happen again.

*

Kristen was closing the windows in the back of the house when she heard a car speed away for the second time that night. She thought about calling the police, but that only made her think of Dani. She was still trying to digest the image of the sexy deputy at her door, who turned out to be the last person on earth she ever thought she'd see in a uniform and the one person she had tried to avoid since arriving in Cypress Lake.

She smiled, remembering their childhood together. They'd been inseparable from the time they were five years old, playing kid games. They spent their childhood through their teenage years swimming and fishing in the lake, and trading stories about what they wanted to be when they grew up. So much had changed since she'd left town. The differences in her and Dani's personalities were like day and night. She had no idea who the woman in the uniform was. One thing was certain; Dani wasn't going to let the past go. The passion in Dani's green eyes used to stir her, but the anger she'd seen in them earlier had startled her.

Thinking about Dani and her uniform brought her back to reality. She'd been at the door because of the dead body in the water. Kristen shivered, recalling the grotesque images of the man's chewed up face and the jagged cut on his neck.

Chapter 5

Dani was floating on her back in the lake under the hot sun. She felt a hand on her face and smiled, opening her eyes to see the face of her skinny orange cat, who was standing on her chest with his paw on her cheek, sniffing her face. She flung him off her and sat up, rubbing the effects of the dream from her face. The alarm on the nightstand buzzed loudly. Shaking her head, she turned it off and stepped into the shower.

A few minutes later, she was dressed in her uniform and heading out the door with bottle of water, an apple, and a banana in her hand. The cat meowed and jumped up on the kitchen table against the wall by the door. She juggled her hands, trying to open the door as she grabbed her keys from the table.

"Oh, no you don't. I've just about had it with you ruining my dreams, cat. You're not my alarm clock. Get your own snacks," she growled, walking out the door.

*

Dani pulled her SUV off the road and slightly into the grass in front of the white house. She threw it into park and climbed out, adjusting her utility belt as she walked up the driveway. She pulled the screen back and knocked hard on the front door as she removed her sunglasses and turned the volume down on the radio attached to her belt.

A minute later, the lock clicked, and the door swung open.

*

Kristen was standing in the kitchen about to cut open a grapefruit when she heard the screen squeak on the front door. The loud tapping that followed made her drop the knife she was holding into the sink. She wiped her hands on the dishtowel and walked through the living room to look through the peep hole.

"Here we go again," she sighed, pulling the door open when she saw the familiar face.

"I'm sorry to bother you. I just wanted to check on you again. I saw the sheriff's office ride by last night. I'm glad they're checking on you too. Did they find out anything yet?"

"I'm fine, Mrs. Cranston. Thank you for checking on me and no, I haven't heard anything from the police. I'm not even sure if I will," Kristen said to her nosy old neighbor.

The woman had driven her family nuts for years, complaining constantly about every renter that had rented their house over the years. She had been on Kristen's doorstep wanting to know what was going on as soon as the last police car had left the day before. Kristen simply told her that someone had drowned and washed ashore on her property. There was no need to tell her that the man had been murdered.

"It's a shame about that young man. I'll pray for his family at church tonight," the old woman said.

"That's a good thing to do, Mrs. Cranston." Kristen forced a smile.

"Did you tell your parents? Oh …" She shook her head. "I bet your mother is just torn up about all of this."

You old twit, maybe you'll be next. Kristen faked a grin. "I called them last night. They were sorry to hear about it, but unfortunately, people drown in the lake every year. He was probably drunk and fell out of his fishing boat."

Kristen's cell phone rang before the nosy neighbor could speak.

"I'd better get that. It could be the sheriff's office. Have a good day, Mrs. Cranston," Kristen said, closing the door.

She pushed the button to send the call to her voicemail box as she picked the knife up out of the sink and sliced through the grapefruit.

*

"Dani Ricketts? Is that you behind that strapping uniform?" the older woman said, opening her screen door.

"Yes, ma'am. I'm here on official Sheriff's Office business, Mrs. Davis," Dani replied.

"Come in," she said, holding the door open.

Dani stepped inside. The single story, crème colored house, had dark wood floors with colorful throw rugs under the tables and in front of the floral printed couch and love seat. An old, worn leather recliner sat in the corner near the TV. Various family photos in mismatched frames adorned the walls of the living room.

"Would you like some coffee?" Mrs. Davis asked.

"No, thanks. When's the last time you or your husband saw Paul?"

"What's he done now?" Mr. Davis questioned as he walked into the room. "That boy isn't worth the sense God gave him," he finished, shaking his head.

Dani cleared her throat. "He was found dead yesterday. I'm sorry."

"Oh my God!" Mrs. Davis put her hand on her chest.

"He overdosed on those damn drugs, didn't he?" Mr. Davis shook his head and wrapped his arms around his wife.

"No. Well, the toxicology results won't be back for another week and a half, so we're not sure if there were drugs in his system, but his death was ruled a homicide."

"What?" Mrs. Davis asked, turning back towards Dani, wiping the tears from her face.

"He was killed by someone."

"What ... how? By who?" Mr. Davis questioned.

"At this point, Mr. Davis, all we know is someone ..." she paused, wondering how much she should tell them. "He was in some kind of altercation, and it resulted in his death. We're not sure of the exact details. It's still very early in the investigation."

"One of those damn drugs dealers probably shot him," Mr. Davis said, shaking his head.

"He wasn't shot, actually. His ... someone ..." she sighed. Dani loathed this part of her job. "His throat was cut," she finally said.

"Oh lord," Mrs. Davis put her hand over her mouth in shock.

"I'm very sorry," Dani murmured.

"Chief, I know he wasn't the best citizen of this town, but he was my boy, and he didn't deserve to die like that. I know he made a lot of enemies, but I hope you'll do everything you can to find the person that did this to him."

"Yes, sir, Mr. Davis. We're working on it as we speak. Keeping crime off the streets of Cypress Lake is our top priority. If you don't mind, I'd like to ask you a few questions that may help us with our investigation."

"Sure. We haven't seen him much, but I'll try to answer anything I can."

"You've mentioned drugs a few times. What do you know about Paul's drug use?"

"The last time we saw him he was strung out on something and asking for money. I know he was on and off the streets for the last few years. We'd give him money to clean himself up and he'd disappear for the better part of a year before coming back for more. This last time …" he stopped, looking at his wife. "He was here about two months ago and I told him that was the last time I ever wanted to see him again. He swore he was clean, but I knew what he looked like when he was high or needed a fix and that's exactly how he looked."

"Do you know where he was getting the drugs? Was he hanging around anyone?"

"He worked with Roger Fillmore from time to time at his lawn service. They'd been friends since middle school. I caught them getting high together in our garage when they were in school. I think that's about the time it all started for Paul."

Dani made a few notes on the pad from her pocket.

"I remember Paul mentioning something about going to the city with Roger when he was here."

"Good," Dani nodded, writing more notes. "If you can think of anything else, please call me," she said, scribbling her cell number on her business card and handing it to him.

"I guess we need to call the funeral home."

"Can I talk to you outside, Mr. Davis?" Dani asked.

"Sure," he said, stepping out behind her and closing the door.

"Are you planning to have him cremated?" she asked.

"No. We have family plots in the cemetery. Why?"

"You'll need to have a closed casket," she paused. "Paul's body was found in the lake and human flesh doesn't hold up well to elements in the water."

He sighed. "I understand."

"His body is at the hospital. You will just need to authorize the funeral home to pick it up and Dr. Harper will release it."

"Okay."

Dani shook his hand and slid her sunglasses on as she walked to her SUV. She tore open her banana as she drove across the small town towards the lake and the house that she had no desire to go back to. Modest sized houses passed the window one by one as she rode down the large road that circled the lake. She pulled up in front of the house with the blue car in the driveway as she swallowed the last bite of banana.

"Damn," she muttered, looking for a place to put the peel. Shrugging, she tossed it over her computer and into the passenger floorboard.

*

Kristen was scanning the internet on her laptop when knocking on the front door grabbed her attention. She looked at the clock on the wall. It was close to lunchtime, and she figured her nosy neighbor was back again.

"This woman's going to drive me insane," she whispered, pulling the door open. "I'm fine. You don't need to check on me every couple of hours," Kristen said, not realizing who was at the door.

Dani pulled the screen open. "I'm not here checking on you. I need to ask you some more questions."

"Come in," Kristen huffed. "I thought you were Mrs. Cranston. That woman drives me nuts."

"They still live next door?" Dani raised an eyebrow.

"Yep."

Dani watched her as Kristen walked across the room and pushed the laptop on the dining table closed. Her feet were bare, and she was dressed in short jean shorts that drew Dani's eyes to her tan legs, and a white tank top that stretched across her round breasts, accentuating her lithe figure. Her hair was haphazardly pulled up off her shoulders in a clip with a few loose strands hanging down here and there and tousled bangs laying lazily on the side of her forehead. She looked somewhat disheveled, yet right at home, and sexy as hell. Dani peeled her eyes away, chiding herself for letting her vulnerability slip as she rested her hands on her utility belt.

"Do you have any new information?" Kristen asked, walking back to the living room.

She was still surprised at the woman Dani had grown into. Kristen avoided her alluring green eyes at all costs, but the uniform Dani wore fit her snugly, highlighting the muscles of her athletic body. Kristen felt the butterflies flutter low in her belly with temptation. It had always been difficult for her to control her attraction to Dani when they were younger, but the woman standing in front of her with the devilish good looks and sinful grin nearly sent her over the edge. She turned around and walked into the kitchen, contemplating sticking her head in the freezer to cool off.

"I know the identity of the man you found," Dani said, peering around the room.

"Oh really? Who was it?" Kristen asked, pouring a glass of ice water.

"I thought you were packing?" Dani countered.

"Not at the moment," Kristen answered.

Dani nodded.

"Are you going to tell me who the dead guy was?"

"Are you sure you don't already know?"

"What's that supposed to mean?"

"When's the last time you saw Paul Davis?" Dani questioned.

"Paul Davis?" Kristen repeated the name with a raised eyebrow before her face sunk slightly. She turned her eyes to the window, looking out at the lake in the distance. "Was that him?"

"Have you seen him since you've been back in town?"

"God, no. I haven't seen anyone since I left, and you know that."

"How do I know?"

"Because …" Kristen sighed. "You know if I was going to come back for anyone it would've been you."

Dani's chest ached at the admission.

"Why didn't you come back?"

"It's complicated, Dani."

"Damn it, Kristen. I deserve to know the truth. You walked away from us … from *me* … without ever saying another word. Then, you show up here twelve years later with one of our classmates dead in your backyard."

"Do you honestly think I had something to do with his death?" Kristen growled.

"I have no idea. I don't know you anymore."

"Yeah, well I don't know you either and unless the Cypress Lake Sheriff's Office is officially arresting me, this conversation is over."

Dani knew when she was defeated. She didn't actually have the right to stand in Kristen's house and accuse her of the murder, but she was hurting, and she wanted answers that had nothing to do with Paul Davis.

"He was living on the streets and caught up in drugs," Dani sighed. "More than likely, he owed his dealer money or something of the kind," she said as she walked out, pulling the door closed behind her.

Chapter 6

Dani sat in Sheriff Fisher's office eating an apple. The week had finally come to an end, and she was happy to put it behind her.

"I hate that this is a drug related murder, but I don't see anything that convinces me otherwise," he said, flipping through the file in front of him.

"Me either. Everyone I spoke to said he smoked pot and dabble with snorting cocaine and selling drugs over the years."

"I just can't believe someone cut his throat. Usually, drug dealers shoot the person and move on."

"I agree, but there's nothing else to go on. Roger Fillmore said he hadn't seen Paul in at least a year and a half. I don't know how true that is, but again, there's no evidence. Nothing." Dani shrugged, as she chomped on the green apple in her hand. "He didn't seem too surprised that someone had murdered Paul, but then again Roger had always been the smarter of the two, so if he knew anything, he hid it well."

"Do you think Roger did this?"

"Who knows. Maybe Paul owed him drug money. We've caught Roger growing pot on his property a few times. He could have been selling it and using Paul as his bootlegger so to speak."

"That makes sense. Roger was probably smoking half of it and buying coke with the money from the pot he did sell. If that were the case, he'd owe Roger a lot of money."

Sheriff Fisher chewed the corner of his mustache in thought.

"Enough money to cut his throat?" Dani questioned.

"I don't know."

"Roger lives on the lake and could have easily ridden around in his boat and dumped Paul's body near the Malone's dock," she said. "I'd love to have a search warrant for his truck and boat, but with no evidence, there's no warrant and we have no probable cause to go on either. It's all speculation at this point."

"Damn it. Sometimes our own laws come back and bite us in the ass." He shook his head. "Let's keep this between us for now. I'll push the city drug dealer angle to Mayor Olsen. Roger Fillmore may have just gotten away with murder. I don't like this … not at all," he sighed.

Dani tossed her apple core into his trash can. "I'll keep an eye on Roger, but I doubt anything will come of it," she said as she walked out of his office.

*

The next morning, Dani dressed in khaki shorts and a dark brown t-shirt with the word sheriff written across her chest in large yellow capital letters. She pulled a red tackle box from the back of her closet and put her pistol, cell phone, and wallet with her badge inside the top compartment. She grabbed a small cooler from the kitchen counter and the fishing pole by the door on the way out of her apartment and drove down to the marina, parking her SUV in the spot reserved for law enforcement.

"Good morning, Chief," the dock master waved to her.

"Hey, Phil," Dani called back as she climbed aboard the white, eighteen-foot center console boat, with Cypress

Lake Sheriff's Office written in large green and yellow letters on the side, matching the letters on her SUV.

She turned the key, bringing the outboard engine to life and letting it idle to warm up as she stored her tackle box and fishing pole. She turned on the police radio, switching it to the main channel to listen for any calls that may need her attention. It was her weekend off, but in a small town like Cypress Lake, there really wasn't such a thing as having days off. She was on call twenty-four hours a day and seven days a week, although she was rarely bothered on her days out of the station. Most of the department knew she would be out on the sheriff boat fishing anyway, so she was easily accessible.

"The lake trout and largemouth bass have been biting over in the groves," the dock master yelled as she backed the boat out of the slip.

"Thanks!" she yelled back before pushing the throttle down and driving away.

She ran along the shoreline of the lake, slowing past the Malone house, as well as Roger Fillmore's before cutting the engine and tossing the anchor out as she drifted towards the overgrown mangroves on the section of the lake that was unoccupied by houses. The woods were thick with cypress trees and large mountains were off in the distance behind them.

Dani turned the radio volume down, keeping it low enough to hear emergency calls without frightening the fish below. She opened her tackle box, choosing a green and white striped crankbait and tied it to the end of her line. Casting it out towards the water weeds, she worked the lure back towards the boat, reeling it in and moving the pole slightly to make it move around like a baitfish under the water.

After a half hour of casting in different spots with no bites, she changed to a green and silver jerkworm that resembled a baitfish. She jigged back and forth, dragging the fake bait through the vegetation near the bottom of the lake. When the lure reached the boat, she reeled it all the way in and cast it back out. After the third cast her line was hit hard, bending the pole down. Dani jerked back, setting the hook in the fish's mouth as she began reeling it in. The fish fought back and forth, trying to get free as she pulled it closer and closer to her.

"Sweet!" she yelled, leaning over the side to bring the largemouth bass into the boat.

She took the hook out of its mouth and measured the twenty-inch fish on the measuring chart on the top of the gunwale. She took a quick picture of it with her phone before putting it back in the water and casting her line back out to do it all over again.

*

The rest of Dani's day had gone the same way. She'd stopped to eat the sandwich she'd packed for lunch between catching fifteen fish and getting ten more bites. After another slow pass by the two houses on the back of her mind, she reached the marina and re-docked the boat in the reserved slip and reminded the dock master to refill the gas tank. The sheriff's office paid a hefty fee for the marina to not only store their boat, but to also keep it ready to go out at any minute.

Dani arrived at the building that housed her apartment and tucked her pistol into the waistband of her shorts and pulled her shirt down over it as she walked through the back door of her parent's store. Her father was in the office, typing on the computer with his reading glasses on the edge of his nose. She grinned and maneuvered through the back to the double doors that led out to the main area of the store. She grabbed a basket from the nearby rack and began perusing the aisles. She'd forgotten her list, but photographic memory never failed her.

She placed various items into the basket as she mentally went down the list and just about missed the woman walking briskly past her. Dani raised an eyebrow when saw the backside of the woman in jeans that hugged her tight ass. Her eyes rose to the salmon-colored t-shirt and light brown hair settling on her shoulders in loose waves. She cocked her head to the side, biting her bottom lip, as she watched the woman walk.

A light smack to the back of her head broke Dani's sinful train of thought. She spun around to face her father. She grinned sheepishly as he smiled, shaking his head.

"I swear you're just like me. Don't let your mother catch you with your tongue hanging out like that."

Dani rolled her eyes, but she knew what he was talking about. Cindy Ricketts ruled with an iron fist.

"Did you catch anything?" he asked.

"Yeah, it was a pretty good day. I got a few pictures of the big ones. I'll text them to you."

"Don't you sneak out of here without seeing your mom."

"Where is she?" she asked.

"She's around here somewhere. I saw her putting a stock order together a little while ago."

"Okay, I'll look for her."

"While you're at it, do more than just *look* at the pretty girl in the tight jeans. Invite her to dinner or something," he chided with a smile that matched hers.

She laughed. "I know how to ask someone on a date, Dad. Thanks."

*

Kristen hated going to Dani's parents' store, but they owned the only general store in town, and it was a one-stop shop for pretty much everyone in Cypress Lake. She'd gone there one other time since she'd been back and thankfully hadn't been recognized. She was just about finished gathering the few things from her list when she turned down the bread aisle.

The woman standing halfway down on the right side, bending over to pick up a package of flatbreads, was most definitely Dani Ricketts. Kristen's eyes focused on the flexing thigh and calf muscles of her runner's legs and moved up to the fitted t-shirt that stretched across the broad shoulders and narrow waist of her athletic torso. Her short, dark brown hair was up in a ponytail with black sunglasses up on the top of her head. She swallowed the lump in her throat and hurried past her, hoping to go unnoticed.

I have to stop lusting after her every time I see her. She was hot in high school, but did she have to grow up looking like that! The damn church walls would go up in flames if she walked inside! Damn. She thought, shaking off the instant arousal Dani seemed to invoke in her as she walked out of the store with her bags.

I'm here for one reason and one reason only, to put the past behind me and finally move on, away from this place.

*

Dani continued walking around the store, filling up her small basket. She spoke to her mother briefly when she found her on the paper goods aisle and promised to come to dinner the following day. She paid for her items and left without ever seeing the beautiful woman again, which was probably a good thing. She didn't have room on her plate for another conquest at the moment. She was trying to juggle the fact that Kristen Malone was back in town, for some unknown reason, causing her buried feelings to surface, conflicting with the pain and anger that had buried them long ago.

Chapter 7

Two weeks had passed, and the last cold front of the season had arrived, dropping the spring temperatures down to the low forties. The sheriff's office had been quiet ever since they wrote the Davis homicide off as a bad drug deal. His parents understood; they knew the kind of life their son had lived. The mayor of Cypress Lake never questioned the case that Sheriff Fisher laid out for him and subsequently, the town had gone back to normal.

Dani was having the most amusing day that she'd seen in the last ten days. It started that morning when two elderly men got into a rift over breakfast and decided to sword fight with tree limbs in the front yard. Their wives' thought they were going to kill each other, so they called the sheriff's office and Dani had arrived in time to break up the comical argument. She was on her way back to the department to do some paperwork and call it a day when a blue car turned onto the main road without stopping at the stop sign, a few hundred yards in front of her.

Dani hit the switch for the lights and siren and stomped the gas pedal to catch up with the speeding vehicle. She pulled over behind the car, punched the tag number into her computer, and got out before the screen finished loading. She adjusted the brown V-neck sweater she wore over her uniform shirt and rested her hand on the butt of the gun in the holster on her utility belt as she strutted up to the car. Pushing her sunglasses up on her head, she leaned down, peering inside the open window.

She nearly fell over backwards when she saw Kristen's chocolate brown eyes staring back at her and an angry expression on her face.

Dani shook her head. *Great.*

"Care to tell me why you ran the stop sign back there? Or possibly why you're going fifty in a thirty-five?" she asked.

Kristen shrugged.

"You're obviously headed somewhere in a hurry."

"Either give me the damn ticket, Dani, or let me go," Kristen huffed. This was the last thing she needed at the moment. The dark gray car she thought had been following her had disappeared and Dani's SUV had appeared in its place with its blue lights flashing. She'd just about had enough of seeing Dani.

"If I didn't know any better, I'd say you were up to something." Dani grinned.

Kristen knew that devilish smile all too well. She turned her face towards the windshield, blowing out a frustrating breath.

"I'm going to let you go … this time, but you need to slow down. This isn't the city," Dani said, pulling her sunglasses back down as she walked away.

She watched Kristen's car drive away as she read over the clean driving record she knew she'd see on the screen.

*

Two days later, Dani was passed out on her couch with the TV across from her playing reruns of Gilligan's Island when her cell phone rang, waking her.

"Sheriff?" she asked, noticing the caller ID as she sat up, stretching her cramped muscles. She was surprised she'd fallen asleep.

"Sorry to wake you, but we have a 10-35 out at Barber's," he said.

Dani was as familiar with the all-you-can-eat diner as the rest of the town, but at three a.m. the eatery was still closed. "What's going on?" she asked, walking across her tiny apartment to her closet.

"Adam pulled into the parking lot to check on a truck that hadn't moved all night and found a man in the driver's seat with a hole in the side of his head. He said it looks like a suicide."

"Damn," she said. "I'm on the way. Tell him not to touch anything."

"There's one more thing," he added. "The truck is registered to Roger Fillmore."

"Holy shit. Is it him inside?"

"I don't know."

"What the hell is going on around here?" she replied, pulling her jeans on.

"I have no idea, but we better get to the bottom of it before it gets out of hand. Call me as soon as you have something. I'm sending Vince to the scene too," he said, hanging up.

Dani hung up the phone and pulled her sneakers on. She tucked her pistol into the waistband of her jeans and grabbed the dark brown jacket that went with her uniform and had the word sheriff stitched across the back in large yellow capital letters, her rank and last name were stitched on the front left breast and a Cypress Lake Sheriff's Office badge was stitched on the opposite side. She slipped it on over her black t-shirt and headed out the door.

*

Dani pulled into the parking lot next to Adam's car and cut the engine on her SUV. She pulled out a pair of gloves and a flashlight from the back of her vehicle and walked over to the silver truck.

"It looks like a suicide," Adam said, pointing to the hole in the left side of the man's head.

Dani walked around and pulled the passenger side door open, shining her light all around the interior of the truck, before walking back to the driver's side.

"I don't see the gun and the entrance wound looks a little odd. I don't think this is a suicide. Here, hold my light." She took her phone from her pocket and began taking pictures of the scene, starting with the entire truck and working her way towards the wound itself.

Vince arrived at the same time as Henry.

"Ouch," Vince said, looking at the body in the front seat of the truck.

"Pull that door open Vince," Dani said, taking more pictures of the full body position inside of the truck before putting her phone away and donning her flashlight again, shining it all over the interior and on the ground.

The man was still in his seat belt, meaning he hadn't been there long when the shot was fired and there was no weapon. The entrance wound was just above the back of his ear and there was no exit wound, meaning the bullet was still in his head. Dani pulled her notepad out of her jacket pocket and began taking notes.

"Start looking for a shell casing," she said to the two deputies.

Henry pulled a pencil from his truck and stuck it into the small bullet hole with the eraser end first. The tip of the pencil pointed at an odd angle away from his body. He pursed his lips, looking at Dani who snapped a photo of the pencil.

"It's not the best tool to use, but we needed to see the bullet angle."

"It's a defensive wound. He jerked his body and turned his head like this because someone pointed a gun at him and pulled the trigger. His seat belt kept him in position, making it like shooting a fish in a barrel for whoever did this."

"I agree," Henry said, removing the pencil and sticking it into a plastic bag. "Are you ready to get him out?" he asked.

"Yeah. I'm hoping he has his wallet in his back pocket," she replied.

Henry walked over to his van and returned with a gurney. Dani unzipped the black bag on the top, laying it open.

"Vince, come help us move him," she yelled.

The three of them maneuvered the body into the bag and Dani pulled the wallet from his back pocket before Henry zipped the bag. He stopped short of closing the bag so that Dani could hold the man's driver's license next to his face. It was a match for the picture on the ID.

"Thanks, Henry. I'll check in with you later," she said.

Henry nodded, closing the bag and buckling the straps across the body.

Dani shook her head and walked over to her SUV. Removing her gloves, she pressed the last call button on her phone and waited as it rang.

"Ricketts? Did you find out anything?" Sheriff Fisher asked, groggily.

"It's Roger Fillmore and it's not a suicide."

"Son of a bitch. I had a feeling you were going to say that. I'll be there in a few minutes."

"Alright. Henry is leaving now with the body."

Dani ended the call and donned a new pair of gloves before walking back to the truck. She went through the glove compartment and center console, looking for anything that would indicate who he met and why, but she found nothing except for receipts for his lawn service customers.

"We've searched every inch of the area," Adam said. "There aren't any shell casings or tire tracks."

"Call the tow service and have them take the truck back to the station. Follow behind them and log it into evidence, and then get back on patrol," she replied.

Dani took her gloves off and tucked a few strands of hair behind her left ear. She'd forgotten to put it up when she'd left in haste and although she had a hair tie in her SUV, she hadn't bothered messing with it.

"Do you think these two murders are linked?" Sheriff Fisher asked, walking up to her.

Dani shrugged. "If they were tied to the same drug deal or possible dealer, then … yeah, but there isn't much to go on."

Sheriff Fisher stuffed his hands into the pockets of his jeans as he watched the wrecker driver load the silver truck.

"The Mayor's going to lose it," he sighed.

"Keep playing the drug angle," Dani said, looking at him.

"I guess this ends our theory about Roger killing Paul."

"Not exactly," she countered, pursing her lips. "Whatever this is … it's bigger than both of them. Maybe they've been dealing drugs in the city. Since we know Paul had a coke habit, it's possible that he made a large dope deal and used the money to snort coke. Roger would've been pissed and could've gotten rid of him. Then, the person who made the deal could've come after Paul when he didn't get the product."

"That makes sense, but at this point, we don't have anything except theories. Has the tox screen come back on Paul yet?"

"No. I'll check on it later when Henry finishes the autopsy. The bullet should still be in his head, since there was no exit wound. Let's hope it's intact and we can match it in the system."

Sheriff Fisher sighed. This was the last thing his sleepy little town needed. In the ten years that he'd been sheriff he'd only had two other homicides. One was a wife who'd shot her cheating husband, and the other was a man who'd stabbed another man to death in a drunken brawl.

"You don't suppose that Malone woman had anything to do with this do you?" he asked.

Dani raised an eyebrow. "Kristen?" She shook her head. "No, there's no motive. I think Paul's body was found at her dock by coincidence. Whoever dumped it there thought the place was vacant. Which, it had been for several weeks over the winter, until she arrived back in town a few weeks ago."

"I know I'm grasping at straws, but at this point we're sitting ducks. It won't hurt to see what she knows about Roger Fillmore."

"We went to school with him and Paul, but she's been gone from Cypress Lake a long time. I doubt she knows anything, but I'll swing by on my way home. Henry should have something for us before lunchtime."

"Sounds good. I'll see you back at the station later. Let me know if you find out anything. I need to brief the mayor," he said climbing into his SUV that matched hers.

*

Dani watched the orange rays of the sun start to peak through the woods and mountains on the horizon, in the distance. The last place she wanted to be was standing on Kristen's doorstep. She knocked on the door a second time, tucked her loose hair behind her left ear and shoved her hands into the pockets of her jeans.

"Dani?" Kristen squinted and yawned, opening the screen door. She ran a hand through her tousled hair and pulled her dark blue robe a little tighter around her naked body. "What are you doing here at the crack of dawn?" she asked, taking in Dani's attire. She looked much younger out of her uniform.

"When's the last time you saw Roger Fillmore?" Dani questioned as she stepped inside.

"Roger? I don't know. High school probably. Why?"

"He was found dead in his truck a few hours ago."

"What! Oh my God," Kristen sat on the couch, shaking her head.

"You know he and Paul were friends. Are you sure you haven't seen either of them since you returned?" Dani tried to avoid the feelings that Kristen's disheveled state stirred deep inside of her.

"No." Kristen stared at the floor.

"What are you hiding from me, Kristen?"

"Nothing," she answered.

Dani's cell phone rang, dragging her attention away from the woman on the couch. "Call me when you decide you're ready to talk," she said as she pulled her phone from her pocket and walked out the door.

"Get over to Roger's house as soon as you get a chance. We have probable cause to search his property and go through his business records. Maybe this will give us the link we're looking for," Sheriff Fisher said after she answered.

Dani started her SUV and pulled out onto the main road. "I just left Kristen Malone's. She said she hasn't seen neither Paul nor Roger since high school."

"Alright. It was a long shot anyway. Wilbur is meeting you at Roger's to help with the search."

"Tell him to give me about thirty minutes. I'm headed home now to change into my uniform. Did you inform Roger's family? I'm not sure if his parents are still in town."

"The next of kin listed on his license is Patty Fillmore. Perry's on his way to her house now."

"She's his ex-wife," Dani said. "I'll get over there to question her after I finish the search." She pulled into the parking lot behind the store and waved at her father who was unloading a delivery from one of his suppliers. She got out of her truck, taking the stairs two at a time up to her apartment.

Chapter 8

Dani spent two hours going through Roger's belongings. She checked every single drawer, cabinet, and closet in his small two-bedroom house. His business records weren't exactly perfect, but they were organized enough for her to get an idea of the order they were filed in the two-drawer cabinet next to his dining room table that doubled as his work desk and home office area. His bank statements showed monthly check deposits and a bunch of cash withdrawals. She ran her finger down the list of lawn customers, hand-written in his record book, gasping when she saw Kristen Malone's address and the name Malone Family scribbled next to it.

She traced the address back as far as four years, noting the quarterly bill had always been paid on time and by personal check. The most recent payment had been received two weeks ago. Dani gathered all the business papers relating to Kristen's house and took them out to her truck. She was unable to find anything with Paul's name on it, but his calendar had the name Mary Jane written in the box for yesterday's date.

"I searched the shed and utility room. I bagged the knives I found in the two tackle boxes. The boat was pretty clean, but I did get some samples of tiny stains that could be dried blood. I put everything in the evidence box in your truck," Wilbur said.

"Good. Did you check the lawn trailer?"

"Yeah. There's nothing in there, except lawn equipment and an old toolbox full of tools."

"Okay. I'm finished with the house. I didn't find much either, only a few bank statements and customer lists for his business. Head back on patrol. I'll call you if I need help with anything else," she said, before climbing back into her SUV. She pulled up the address for Patty Fillmore that the sheriff had emailed to her and headed off in that direction.

*

Dani knocked on the door and rested her hands on her utility belt while she waited for someone to answer. A petite blond dressed in a t-shirt and jeans finally answered. Her face was flushed, and her eyes were red. She'd obviously been crying.

"Hey, Patty. I hate to bother you today, but I need to ask you some questions," Dani said.

"It's fine. Come in. Do you want something to drink?" Patty asked.

"No, thanks." Dani followed her inside and took a seat on the chair adjacent to the sofa as she opened the notepad she carried.

"I can't believe this," Patty ran her hand through her head.

"When is the last time you saw Roger?"

"We see each other around town here and there, but I haven't had a conversation with him in five or six months. We've been divorced for almost three years."

"Did you see him in town recently?"

Patty thought about it. "I don't know. I don't think so. He doesn't go to church anymore. I think the last time I saw him was probably a month ago at your parent's store."

"Did he mention anything about going to the city?"

"No. We said a quick hello and moved on. He started going to the city a lot before we got divorced though. That's when I realized his drug business was more important than I was."

"Was he a user?"

"He smoked pot from time to time, but it wasn't an everyday occurrence."

"When's the last time you saw Paul Davis?"

"Paul? I read in the paper that he died a few weeks ago. Was he murdered too?"

"Yes."

"Oh my God. Do you think the same person killed them both?"

"I can't talk about either case because it's an ongoing investigation. Did you see Paul recently?"

"No. I haven't seen Paul since right after my divorce. You know he and Roger have been best friends since they were kids, but Paul's been in and out of trouble and I blame him for bringing Roger down to his level. When they started selling drugs in the city, I gave Roger an ultimatum and he obviously didn't choose me."

"When you were married, did he ever mention where he went in the city or maybe a name?"

"No. He never talked to me about any of that stuff. I knew this was going to come back to bite him in the ass one day," she wiped a tear from her face. "I tried to tell him to stay away from Paul."

"So, you think Paul had something to do with his death?"

"Oh, I'd bet money on it. Paul probably screwed some big dealer over in the city and they paid with their lives. He wasn't the brightest crayon in the box to begin with and once he started snorting coke, he went further downhill.

Roger used to say he was useless as tits on a bull at work because of his drug habit."

"Do you happen to own any guns?"

"I have a shotgun that I keep under my bed. Do you need to see it?"

"No. That won't be necessary. Here's my card with my cell number. Call me if you think of anything else," Dani said, walking towards the door.

She sat in her truck for a minute writing a few additional notes before driving back across town towards the lake.

*

Kristen was about to back out of her driveway when a white sheriff's office SUV pulled up across the end of the driveway, blocking her in. She blew out a frustrated breath and shut the engine off. Dani was walking towards her, dressed in her uniform once again, as she climbed out of the car.

"What now?" Kristen growled.

"We need to talk."

"I don't have time for this."

"Well, as of right now, you're my only suspect, so you better make time for it. I've just about had enough of your little dog and pony show. You need to tell me the truth right now," Dani sneered.

"What the hell are you talking about?" Kristen countered.

Dani nodded towards the neighbor's house at the open window.

"Oh, for Christ's sake! Come into the house," she said, unlocking the door.

Dani walked inside behind her, shutting the front door.

"You can't possibly be serious. You actually think I killed Paul and Roger?"

"You tell me."

"Dani," Kristen said, looking at her.

"You lied to me this morning and I want to know why. I know you're hiding something. I'm not Dudley fucking Do-Right and if you keep treating me like I am, I'll run your ass down to the station and we can do this there."

"I'm not hiding anything, and I didn't lie to you. What the hell are you talking about?" Kristen huffed as she crossed her arms.

"You haven't talked to Roger Fillmore since high school, isn't that what you told me this morning?"

"Yes. I haven't talked to anyone in this town since I moved away, except for you and the other officer that was here when I found Paul's body."

"You've been paying Roger Fillmore to cut the grass here for the past four years. How do you explain that?"

"Roger? My father hired a company called Cypress Landscaping to care for the property a while ago and when he transferred the deed for the house to me two years ago, I simply kept the same company."

"Roger Fillmore owned Cypress Landscaping. In fact, he's the one that'd been physically mowing your lawn. Actually, he and Paul were because at one time Paul worked for him. You're telling me you knew nothing about this?"

"No." Kristen stepped back. "I had no idea and if I did, he wouldn't have been doing our lawn any longer," she added, shaking her head.

"Why not?"

"It's a long story that I don't have time for right now, Dani."

"Damn it, Kristen. I wish you'd just tell me what the hell is going on." Dani walked back over to the door. "Don't leave town until this gets straightened out. That's coming from the sheriff, not me," she said, before leaving.

Kristen watched her walk down the driveway before flopping down on the couch. *Shit.* Things had gotten way out of hand, and she had no idea how to regain control. Seeing Dani wasn't helping matters. The more she saw her, the more she wanted her, and she didn't have time for distractions or strolls down memory lane. She had wanted to explain everything to Dani on more than one occasion, but the timing had never been right and there was no sense in dragging her into the mess anyway.

She walked into her bedroom and loaded the pistol she kept under her mattress.

*

Dani walked into the sheriff's office and tore open a banana as she sat down across from him.

"Did you get over to Henry's yet?" he asked.

"Son of a bitch," she squawked.

Sheriff Fisher shook his head.

"I found out Kristen Malone was one of Roger's lawn customers. I think it's a coincidence, but I questioned her anyway. She said she didn't know he was the owner."

"Do you believe her?"

"I don't know, but I just don't think she did any of this. What would her motive be?"

"Maybe she's a scorned lover," Sheriff Fisher shrugged.

Dani shook her head. That was one thing she knew for sure. Kristen was definitely not interested in men. "You've been watching too much cable TV," she laughed. "Kristen hasn't seen anyone here since high school. I think she's just caught up in the wrong place at the wrong time."

"Keep an eye on her anyway. She's our only suspect at this point."

"I know. Roger's ex-wife, Patty, reiterated the drug angle. Roger's affiliation with Paul and pushing drugs in the city were the reasons behind her divorce."

"Did you find any connection to the city in Roger's stuff?"

"Nope. Well, nothing except the words *Mary Jane* written on his calendar the day he died. It could be that he was doing a pot deal in the parking lot, and it went south."

"That's right on track with your drug dealer theory. Mayor Olsen is talking on the morning news tomorrow and he plans to touch on the subject of the two recent drug-related murders. Let's hope this is the end of the trail."

*

Dani walked into the hospital, yawning like a lazy dog.

"You're too young to be doing that this early," Henry smiled, checking the clock on the wall.

Dani grinned. "Yeah, well this spring chicken's been up and working for almost fourteen hours."

"Me too. Well, I did take a power nap after I finished your body from this morning. Digging the smashed-up bullet from someone's head was the perfect way to spend my day off," he said sarcastically. "If these murders keep up, I may have to hire an assistant."

"Let's hope this was the last one or I may be looking for a new job," she teased.

He slid a blue folder over to her. "That's the toxicology report on the last guy."

Dani opened it, flipping through the three-page report on Paul Davis. He'd had both marijuana and cocaine in his system when he died.

"It's hard to say how much time passed between absorbing the drugs and time of death, but I'd say he was definitely high when he was killed. Cocaine doesn't stay in the system long and the levels in his blood were the highest I've ever seen."

"High enough to not know what was going on?" she asked.

"Most likely." He nodded. "That's probably why there were no defensive wounds. He was too high to fight back."

"I had a feeling you were going to say that. What about the one from this morning?"

Henry handed her a small glass jar with shards of metal in the bottom of it.

"That's the bullet. It fragmented into three pieces."

"Wonderful," she said tipping the bottle. The chunks rattle against the glass.

"Based on the size of the entrance wound, I'd say it was probably a .380 caliber, but it could be a 9mm, and the path of the bullet definitely points to a defensive position like we talked about at the scene. He probably saw the gun and turned away, but his seatbelt held him still long enough for the bullet to hit him."

"Great. Got anymore useless news for me?"

"Nope."

"Let me know when you get his tox screen back, although, I doubt it'll help," she said as she left.

Chapter 9

A week later, Dani sat at her small kitchen table, cleaning her .45 caliber service handgun and the 9mm revolver that she'd had for years and used as her backup pistol. She thought about the bullet in the glass bottle sitting on her desk at the station. Henry had said it was either a .380 or a 9mm, both of which were the most popular concealed carry calibers, which made it nearly impossible for anyone to figure out exactly whose gun had delivered the fatal shot to Roger Fillmore's head.

Her skinny orange cat leapt up onto the opposite end of the small table, eyeing her suspiciously.

"What do you want, cat? I'm glad you can't talk. You'd have so much to say you'd probably never shut up." She put her service gun back into the holster on her belt, set her smaller pistol on her nightstand next to the wallet that held her badge, and tossed some snacks on the floor for him.

A soft knock on the door grabbed her attention. She checked the peephole and pulled the door open.

"Hey, Dad."

"I saw the mayor's speech on the news the other night. How bad is it?" he asked, hugging her before sitting on the couch.

"Paul and Roger were both in over their heads with drug dealing and Paul was a user himself. We're pretty sure it's tied to the city, just as the mayor said."

"I hope you're right. The last thing we need around here is a murderer on the loose. Your mothers already worried to death about you, and we keep hearing people talking about it in the store. I think the town's a little more worried than the mayor thinks."

"I'm fine."

"I know that. Hell, I paid for you to have a higher education than all those idiots you work with put together. Just be safe and watch your back. That's all that I'm saying."

Dani smiled. "I'm going fishing in the morning to celebrate my first day off in ten days. Do you want to go?"

"Nah, we have inventory next week and I'm still doing pre-counts," he said, petting the cat as it rubbed against his leg.

"Do you want some help?"

"No. You gave the store enough of your youth. Go fishing and enjoy your day off."

*

Kristen was sitting on edge of the dock with her legs dangling over the side. The last cold spell had finally departed and the warm weather behind it was welcoming. She thought briefly about the dead body that had been found a few feet away. The photos of Paul's half eaten face made her shiver. She stood up and walked to the end of the dock, distancing herself from that spot by the rocks before sitting back down. The noise of a boat motoring nearby grabbed her attention. She was wearing sunglasses, but squinted anyway in the bright sun, and was able to make out the words *Sheriff's Office* written on the side of the white vessel. The boat drifted a little closer and she strained her eyes to see who was in it, wondering if it was Dani.

Simply thinking of the woman elevated her heartbeat. The biggest mistake she'd ever made was not coming back for Dani after her family had moved away abruptly. So many years had passed between them, and she wondered if Dani would understand the reasons why she had chosen to stay away and the reasons why she had returned.

Kristen wasn't sure if she could handle seeing her again. The only thing they'd managed to do in the past month was quarrel and when Dani appeared at her door flashing her wild green eyes and devilish grin, the last thing she wanted to do was argue. She'd spent many nights peeling Dani out of her sheriff's uniform, layer by layer, in her dreams, leaving her restless and aroused.

Whether she could handle it or not, she didn't want to see Dani again. Too many emotions were stirred and she was in Cypress Lake for one reason only and Dani Ricketts wasn't going to spoil her plan. Kristen stood and turned to walk back up to the house.

*

When she finished fishing, Dani cruised around the lake like she always did when she was out on the water. The warm weather had brought many people out of their homes, onto their docks, and into their boats. She returned waves and nods as she rode by. She wasn't working, so didn't bother checking registrations as she passed other boaters.

She slowed as she neared the section of the lake that she'd purposely avoided all morning. She didn't need binoculars to know the woman sitting on the end of the dock was Kristen. She had changed a little here and there over the years, seemingly growing up, but there was no mistaking the chocolate brown eyes and adorable smile that grabbed her attention when Dani had been only five years old. She remembered the day like it was yesterday.

The new girl in the class had been told to pick an empty seat and after looking at all the kids in the room, she had chosen the one next to Dani. They had become instant friends and on Dani's sixth birthday, Kristen had kissed her cheek and told her she would always be her best friend. Then, on Dani's sixteenth birthday, Kristen kissed her lips and told her she would always love her.

Dani always hoped she'd see Kristen again, she just hadn't been prepared for the way it would affect her after all these years. So much had changed in their lives. She was the chief deputy for the sheriff's office, in the middle of a double murder investigation and ironically, the only suspect was the woman who'd fled from her life without so much as a goodbye and mysteriously returned without so much as a hello.

Dani shook her head. She was about to gun the engine and head back to the marina when she saw Kristen stand up and turn away. She bumped the throttle into gear and motored closer.

*

Kristen had barely taken three steps when she heard the boat motor growing closer. *Shit.* She spun on her heels as the boat drifted close to the dock. Dani was dressed in a sheriff's office t-shirt and khaki shorts that clung nicely to her athletic curves. Her hair was pulled back in a short ponytail and dark sunglasses covered her eyes.

"What can I do for you, deputy?" Kristen put a little too much emphasis on the last word as she crossed her arms.

Dani bit back the grin that formed on her mouth at the sight of Kristen in a tight t-shirt and cut-off jean shorts. Her honey brown hair fell in loose waves around her neck and the top of her shoulders, revealing gold hoop earrings that were about the diameter of a quarter.

"Are you ready to talk?" Dani asked, reaching over to keep the boat from bumping into the wooden dock.

"Not really," Kristen said, running her hand through her hair and pushing her long bangs to the side. "Unless you're here to arrest me."

"Should I be? Is there something you need to tell me?" Dani questioned.

"Nope."

"Good. I was hoping maybe you'd want to talk and not about my case. I haven't seen you in twelve years. There's a lot to talk about."

"You need to let it go, Dani." She looked down at the water, and then back at her. "I have," she finished.

"You mean let *you* go. Don't worry, I did that a long time ago," she sighed inwardly. "We were best friends once, although I think you've forgotten that," Dani said wistfully as she pushed off from the dock and moved back to the controls.

The white boat sped away, disappearing across the lake. Kristen wiped the couple of tears from her cheek as she walked back to the house.

Chapter 10

Two days later, Dani was sitting in the mayor's office with Sheriff Fisher in the chair next to her.

"I don't think I need to stress to the two of you how important it is to close this case. The people of this town are already talking and many of them are starting to feel frightened in their own homes," Mayor Olsen stated, rubbing his beard in thought. "We've buried two of our citizens and I don't plan on burying a third."

"Yes, sir, we're working every angle of the case and everything we come across leads us right back to drugs and drug deals," Sheriff Fisher replied.

"Damn it, I know that. The point I'm trying to get at is we need to shut this drug ring down. If we get the drugs out of Cypress Lake, then there won't be a reason for the dealers to come here in the first place."

"That's a great suggestion, Mayor Olsen, but the problem is Paul Davis and Roger Fillmore were dealing and running drugs in the city, and subsequently, the drugs followed them back here. I don't believe we have a drug problem within our town limits," Dani countered.

"Dani, I've known you since you were a kid. Your own mother is one of the concerned citizens voicing their opinions. Can you honestly sit here and tell me that this is over and there won't be any more dead bodies turning up in our town?" he asked sarcastically.

"No sir. I don't think anyone can do that, but it's your job to make these concerned citizens feel safe here in

Cypress Lake and it's our job to actually make them safe," she responded.

Mayor Olsen gritted his teeth. He was coming up on the end of his second three-year term and had planned on running for one more. These unsolved, gruesome murders were throwing a major wrench into his campaign plans and could ruin his chances of being re-elected.

"Someone needs to hang for these crimes, and I suggest you work around the clock until you find the person responsible," he declared with a hint of agitation in his voice. "We'll meet again in two weeks. I expect you both to have something more for me than an untouchable drug dealer in the city."

Dani walked out of his office behind Sheriff Fisher.

"You just pissed him off," Sheriff Fisher uttered, shaking his head.

"I know. He's a pompous ass. What does he expect us to do, cross county lines to find a ghost? Drug dealers and users are a dime a dozen in the city." She shrugged as her cell phone rang with an unknown number.

"Chief Ricketts," she growled.

*

The sadness on Dani's face had been eating away at Kristen over the last few days. She couldn't go on any longer knowing that she was the cause of it, so she dialed the number from the business card on the counter.

"Is this a bad time?" Kristen asked, hearing the anger in Dani's voice.

"Kristen?" Dani questioned, softening her voice as she walked towards her SUV.

"Yeah. I can call you later or—"

"No, it's fine. Is everything okay?"

"Yes. I … are you sure you don't want to call me back? You sound upset."

"I just got out of a meeting with our mayor that didn't go well," she said, starting her vehicle and pulling out of the parking lot of the town hall building. "Anyway, are you okay?"

"I'm fine. Isn't David Olsen the mayor now?"

"Yep, and he's even more of a dickhead now than he used to be when he was the sheriff."

"I never cared for him either."

Dani looked at the phone in her hand and put it back to her ear. She was surprised to be having a regular conversation with the woman on the other end. "Are you sure everything's okay?" she asked again.

"Yes, I'm sorry." She realized Dani must be wondering why she was on the phone. "I called to see if you wanted to come by … maybe for dinner … we could talk," Kristen fumbled.

Dani checked her watch. "I'm downtown at the moment and I need to run home and change clothes, but I can be there in thirty minutes."

"Okay," Kristen replied before hanging up.

Dani ended the call and pressed the gas pedal down a little harder. She had no idea why Kristen wanted to talk suddenly. She was sure the awaiting conversation was going to end in argument, just as their others had, but either way, it was still better than stewing on her couch all night over the lousy meeting.

*

Large rain drops began falling from the dark sky. Dani shoved her hands into the front pockets of her jeans and huddled closer after knocking on the door. She wasn't sure why she was nervous. She'd seen Kristen half a dozen times over the past six weeks. Maybe it was the thought of talking about something other than dead bodies that had her rattled.

Kristen opened the door with a tentative smile on her face, waving for Dani to come in out of the rain.

"I didn't know it was supposed to rain tonight," Kristen said, watching the pouring drops before closing the door.

"Yeah, well it's the perfect end to my shitty day," Dani murmured.

"We can do this another time—"

"No, I'm sorry. I have a lot on my mind right now, but I'm glad you want to talk. I'm curious to hear what you have to say." Dani watched her walk across the living room towards the open kitchen. Kristen was wearing jeans and a pink shirt that hugged her slender body, causing sinful thoughts to creep into Dani's head. Kristen had been cute when they were younger, but she'd grown into a beautiful woman.

Dani grinned, shaking her head as she sat down on the couch. Kristen was no longer hers, but no matter how many times she told herself that, she still wanted her.

"Would you like something to drink? I have beer, wine, and water."

"Beer," Dani nearly shouted. She needed something to calm her down. Her blood pressure was still elevated from the meeting and Kristen's sexy backside wasn't helping to lower it.

Kristen returned to the couch with a beer for Dani and a glass of red wine for herself.

73

"I guess you're probably wondering why you're here."

"A little bit," Dani answered. "Are you finally ready to confess?"

"Confess to what? Those murders?" Kristen sipped her wine and tucked her feet under her. "Are you serious?"

Dani shrugged, taking a long swallow of her beer. "If the shoe fits."

"If you honestly think I killed Paul and Roger then maybe we shouldn't be having this conversation because you obviously don't know me," Kristen huffed.

"You're right. I don't know you … at least not anymore."

"That's why I asked you here. You were right when you said we used to be best friends." She sipped some more of her wine, trying to avoid the green eyes staring back at her. "We've changed so much in the last twelve years."

"I haven't changed that much, but you … you're a completely different person," Dani said.

"You're a damn sheriff's deputy. Who the hell ever thought that would happen?" Kristen shook her head.

Dani shrugged. "I graduated and realized business wasn't for me, so a month into my freshman year I changed my major to criminal justice."

Kristen raised an eyebrow. "You went to college?"

"Of course. I'm not an idiot, Kristen."

"I know that. You were probably the smartest person in our graduating class." Kristen smiled. "I just … I guess I didn't realize you needed to go to college to be Barney Fife."

Dani laughed. It was the sweetest sound that Kristen had heard in years.

"You don't. Actually, all you need to do is graduate from high school and go to the police academy in the city.

Now, if you want to be anything besides a deputy, like sheriff or mayor, then you need a degree in criminal justice."

"Did you have to go to the police academy too?"

"Oh yeah, everyone in law enforcement does. I just went to college first." Dani took another sip from the bottle that was sweating in her hand. "What about you? What do you do?"

"I …" Kristen drank from her glass. "I went to college too, for business actually. I worked odd jobs here and there and finally went back to school a few years ago for real estate and I've been doing that ever since. In fact, I own my own agency in the city."

"Wow, that's … interesting."

"I told you I was here to settle my family's affairs. They sold this house to me two years ago and I'm sick of dealing with the property."

"You said you were packing, but I still don't see any boxes."

"I've been boxing up the stuff in the attic and taking it to a storage unit. My parents aren't sure if they want any of it."

Dani peered around at the living room again. Nothing looked moved from the past few times that she'd been there.

"You look like you want to search the house," Kristen snarled.

"No, I'm just curious. I'm not here as a sheriff's deputy."

"Uh huh." Kristen raised an eyebrow. "You still think I killed them, don't you?"

"No, I don't, but suspicion is hard to ignore."

"Maybe you should leave then."

"Damn it, Kristen, I'm not here on sheriff's office business. You invited me to talk, remember?"

"Fine."

"Where are they living now anyway?" Dani asked, changing the subject.

"Who?" Kristen huffed.

"Your parents."

"In the city."

"Is that where you went when you moved away over night?"

"Yes," Kristen replied, looking away from her.

"What happened?" Dani asked. "You were here one day and gone the next."

"It was complicated, Dani." She sipped the last of her wine. "Hell, it still is."

"Too complicated to tell me? I was so damn in love with you. We were best friends, but we were so much more. At least, I thought we were, and then you disappeared."

"I'm sorry. That's the way it had to be." She paused. "I loved you too, more than anything in this world," she whispered.

"I don't understand why you never even said goodbye. I could've helped you. My family would've helped yours if they needed it. I don't understand why you just vanished without a trace."

"They ..." She blew out a frustrating breath. "My parents ... found out about us. They knew we were sleeping together and ... they took me away from you and cut all ties to Cypress Lake to keep us apart." She stood and walked into the kitchen.

Dani's mind played her words over and over, but it didn't add up. Kristen returned with a fresh glass.

"That doesn't make sense. Your parents liked me. They knew we were close."

"Close, yes, but not lesbian lovers. My mother threw the bible at me, literally."

Dani raised an eyebrow. "I never knew they felt that way."

"They hid a lot of things from everyone."

"Why didn't you come back after you turned eighteen?"

"They threatened to never speak to me again if I contacted you … they almost didn't allow me to go to college. They were afraid I'd come find you."

"Kristen, that's absurd. You were an adult!"

"There's no reason to get upset about it now. It's in the past."

"Past, hell! You tore me apart, Kristen. You could've been dead for all I knew!"

"It wasn't exactly easy for me either. That was the worst time of my life, but I moved on and I grew up, so did you." Kristen walked into the kitchen, setting her empty wine glass on the counter. "You can't change the past, Dani," she said, stepping back into the living room.

Dani stared out the window at the dock in the distance. She could barely see the light at the end through the heavy rain pouring down in the darkness.

"I never meant to hurt you. I did what they wanted me to do because, well, at the time, it was the right thing to do. I regret never trying to see you again," Kristen whispered as she squeezed Dani's hand.

The contact from Kristen's hand on hers felt like lightning rods shooting up Dani's arm, straight to her heart. She could fall back into the past so easily, but she was no longer a teenager without a care in the world and deep down she knew Kristen wasn't being honest with her. Dani pulled her hand away and stood up.

"I need to get going. I've had a long day as it is and Mayor Dickhead thinks we aren't working hard enough, so I'm sure my workload is about to double."

"What about dinner?" Kristen asked, walking to the door with her.

"Another time." Dani smiled.

"It's pouring. Are you sure you want to go out in this mess?"

"I'll be fine. It's not going to let up anytime soon." Dani took half a step forward.

The electricity between them welded Kristen to the ground. She was sure Dani was about to kiss her. Her pulse raced and her breathing literally came to a crashing halt in anticipation, but Dani turned away and walked out to her vehicle.

The heavy rain had soaked Dani to the bone. Her wet clothes slid across the worn leather seat of her SUV. She started the truck and drove away without looking back. If Kristen didn't trust her enough to tell her the truth about why she'd left and chose to stay away all these years, then there was no sense in staying to see where the night might lead. She turned the dispatch radio off and drove home in silence, listening to the rain pelting the roof of her vehicle.

The skinny orange cat meandered up to her when she entered the apartment, sniffing the air before turning his nose up and scampering off.

"Asshole cat," she said, shaking her head as she set her gun on the nightstand next to her bed and peeled out of her wet clothing. "See if I give you any treats," she yelled to him as she turned the shower temperature to hot and pulled the lever. She pulled a clean towel from the cabinet below the sink and set it on the closed toilet seat lid before stepping under the spray.

*

Kristen grabbed the empty beer bottle from the coffee table, tossing it into the kitchen trash on her way to the master bedroom upstairs. She wasn't sure why she was feeling so dejected. It wasn't like she'd actually made a move, and Dani had turned her down. She wasn't even sure she would've acted on it if Dani *had* made a move of her own, but the idea of it made her tingle. Seeing Dani sitting casually on the couch in jeans and a t-shirt, just as she'd done hundreds of times when they were kids, made her forget about all the time that had passed between them. She was kidding herself if she thought Dani wanted more than the answers to the questions that she kept asking. Answers that Kristen wasn't ready to give to her. Not now. Maybe not ever.

Oh, Dani. It's better if you don't know.

*

The next afternoon, Dani was sitting at her desk, staring at her computer and tossing a green apple from hand to hand as she read over the spreadsheet on the screen.

"Sheriff Fisher's looking for you," Vince said, popping his head into her office.

She bit into the apple as she clicked the mouse to go to another screen. "He knows where to find me," she replied, nodding for him to come in.

"Any new information on our killer?" he asked, sitting down across from her.

"Not much."

"Are you sure it's the same person? I mean the M.O. is completely different."

"You're correct," she took another bite, talking as she chewed. "The only thing … those two had … in common was drugs. Whether the murders … are linked … well, I'm going on instinct. I really think … Roger killed Paul … and then some dealer … from the city killed Roger," she finished, tossing the apple core into the trash and taking a long sip of water from the bottle on her desk.

"There you are," Sheriff Fisher said from the doorway.

"I've been right here, working on the schedule most of the day. Someone has to figure out a way to appease his majesty."

Vince got up from the chair across from her desk and walked out of the small room.

"We're burning man hours that we don't have allocated. I've adjusted and readjusted the schedule so many times that I may be working the next thirty days with no time off just to cover shifts."

"I'm going to make an executive decision and say to stay on our regular schedule for now. If Mayor Olsen doesn't like it, then he can find some money in the mediocre budget he gives us to hire more deputies."

"My thoughts exactly," Dani replied, pulling the schedule back up on her computer once again. "I spoke to my contact with the city police department."

"What did he say?"

"Not much. A lot of the dealers on the street use 9mm rounds because they're cheap and easy to get. Without a bullet, it's impossible to match anything. He hasn't heard anyone on the street talking about Cypress Lake, so if Roger's murder is drug related, it was small potatoes."

"Great. How the hell do I go to the mayor with that? 'Mr. Mayor, our case is closed based on it being a small potatoes crime.' He's liable to fire us both," he said, shaking his head.

"Good. I could use a damn day off or even a vacation for that matter. You know he's only being an arrogant asshole because in all the years that he was sheriff, he never saw an actual homicide. Sure, Mrs. Antonio shot her husband, and Olsen had to handle that case, but she was standing in the kitchen with the damn smoking gun in her hand and she'd thought her husband was an intruder at the time."

Sheriff Fisher laughed. "Yeah, I remember that. I'd just moved here and was working as a deputy."

"It's all a political ploy to secure votes. He's more worried about his hairy ass than keeping the people of this town safe. He's always been a selfish prick. I don't understand why people keep voting him back in."

"Me either, but unfortunately, butting heads with him isn't helping matters."

"I really think we need to say Roger killed Paul because he stole drug money from him, then Roger was killed by the dealer that Paul ripped off. Tie that idea up into a nice little package with a bow and call it a day," she said.

"Is that what you think really happened?"

She shrugged. "Do you honestly think we have a murderer on the loose in Cypress Lake?"

"No," he retorted, shaking his head. "I don't think we'll see another murder for the next five years, maybe longer. Those two guys got themselves caught up in a mess and it ended badly for both of them. We'll probably never know exactly how it went down, but at this point, I don't see a reason to keep beating a dead horse. Drugs will kill you … case closed."

Dani chuckled as he walked out of her office.

Chapter 11

A few days later, Dani's day off was coming to a close. She'd spent most of it cleaning her studio apartment, washing clothes, and helping her dad repair one of the dairy freezers in the store. She was tired, but the hot shower she'd taken renewed her energy.

The warm spring sun had finally set, letting a cool breeze drift through town. Dani slipped on a pair of jeans and a t-shirt, preparing to walk down to Muddy's for an early dinner, when her cell phone rang. The unknown number looked vaguely familiar.

"Ricketts," she answered, pulling her sneakers on.

"Dani!"

"Kristen? What's wrong?"

"Someone's in my house!" Kristen said, shakily. "They broke in."

Dani stuffed her pistol into her waistband and snatched her wallet and keys from the nightstand. "I'm on the way. Get out of the house and wait in your car!" She yelled as she took the stairs down to the parking lot two at a time.

"Okay, hurry, Dani. I don't know if he's still in there." Kristen locked herself in her car.

Dani jumped into her SUV and pushed the speaker button on her cell phone as she set it in the console. "Don't hang up, Kristen. I'll be there in two minutes," she replied, stomping the gas pedal and peeling out of the parking lot with the lights and siren blaring.

Dani turned on the dispatch radio and keyed the microphone attached to the side of the computer. "Dispatch, this is Chief Ricketts, we have a 10-31 at 321 Lake Drive. The owner is a friend and called me at home. I'm 10-76, two minutes out."

"Copy, Chief. Deputy Nyman is 10-76, ETA five minutes."

"Copy." Dani set the microphone down. "Kristen, are you still there?"

"Yes."

"I'm turning onto your road now. Have you seen anyone come out?"

"No. I hear your siren."

Dani skidded to a stop in front of the house and jumped out of her SUV with her gun drawn. Kristen opened her car door to get out, but Dani slammed it closed.

"Stay here. When my deputy gets here, tell him I went inside."

"Okay," Kristen said, watching her back as Dani entered the house with her gun in front of her.

"Sheriff's office!" Dani yelled. "Sheriff's office! Come out now!" She flipped the switch for the living room light, noticing the room was disheveled as she walked through to the kitchen and then to the bathroom and finally, the back bedroom, where she found an open window.

She looked in the closet and under the bed, and worked her way up the stairs, checking the far bedroom before going into the master. There was no one in the house, but someone had definitely gone through there looking for something. She looked down at the rumpled comforter on the queen-sized bed. This was obviously where Kristen had been spending her nights since arriving back at the family home.

"Chief!" Wilbur yelled from just inside the front door.

"Up here!" she shouted as she left the room. "All clear," she called, walking down the stairs.

"Get the print kit from your cruiser. I think the window in the front bedroom is the point of entry," she said.

He walked out to his car and informed Kristen to stay put until Dani came to get her. He returned with a pair of gloves for each of them and his fingerprinting kit. They started on the window, dusting for prints, but found nothing usable. After dusting a few open drawers with no luck, Dani stopped him.

"Whoever did this was wearing gloves. Son of a bitch," she growled, walking out the front door and waving for Kristen to come inside as she walked to her SUV.

Kristen was visibly shaken when Dani met her by the car.

"It's alright. Whoever it was is long gone. They tossed the house but didn't leave any prints. It looks like they came in through the front bedroom window and probably left the same way."

"Damn it," Kristen said, wrapping her arms tightly around herself. She walked through the front door, looking at the mess in the living room that she'd seen when she first arrived and called Dani. "Did they do this to all of the rooms?"

"I'm afraid so." Dani removed her rubber gloves. "Do you know what they were looking for?"

"No. There really isn't anything of value here." She shook her head.

"I'm assuming you weren't home when this happened."

"No, I was out," Kristen replied. "I'd just returned and noticed the mess when I walked in. I called you right away."

"Any idea who may have done this?" Dani asked.

"No. I don't know. I didn't think anyone knew I was here." Kristen blew out a frustrating breath and sat down on the couch. "I've seen a dark car a few times that I'd swear was following me."

"When did that start?"

"Remember that night you pulled me over? That was probably the third time I'd noticed it and that's why I was speeding."

"Why didn't you tell me this?"

"Dani." Kristen looked at her. "You and I haven't actually been on speaking terms this entire time and you think I killed Roger and Paul. I didn't think you would believe me."

"I'm the Chief Deputy for the sheriff's office and if that's not enough, I think our history should have made you feel like you could come to me. I'm sorry if I've made you feel otherwise." Dani sat down next to her. "What did the car look like?"

"I don't know. Every time I've seen it, it's been late in the day near dusk. I know it's dark, like I said, gray or blue."

"Two door or four door?"

"I've only seen the side of it once it and it was dark out, but I think it's a four door. It's about the size of my Camry I guess, maybe a little smaller."

Dani made new notes on the notepad she'd retrieved from her truck when she went out to get Kristen.

"You don't think the person that killed Paul and Roger is after me ... do you?"

"No, I don't see a connection. Their deaths are drug related."

"This whole thing is starting to scare the hell out of me."

"Is anything missing that you know of?"

"I didn't really look around," she said, getting off the couch.

Kristen checked each room downstairs before moving to the second floor. She immediately went to the master bedroom and stuck her hand under the corner of the mattress. "Shit!"

"What's wrong?" Dani asked, from the doorway.

"My gun's gone. I forgot to grab it when I left."

"You have a gun?"

"Had. I always carried it with me for protection."

Dani wrote a few more notes. "What kind of gun was it?"

"It's a solid black Taurus .380 caliber. It's small and easy to conceal. I have a permit for it. Well, in the city I do."

Dani raised an eyebrow and made a few extra notes.

"Where did you say you were when this happened?"

"I said I was out. I had errands to run." Kristen eyed her suspiciously. "If you are insinuating that I faked this whole thing and ransacked my own house I'm going to slap the hell out of you. I've just about had enough of you accusing me of things that I've had nothing to do with. Someone is obviously playing games with me. First, there's Paul's body under my dock, then someone starts following me around, and now this," she snarled.

"Kristen, I never said you did this. You're jumping to conclusions. As far as the other stuff, it's a little strange and maybe coincidental, but I have never accused you of anything. I merely said you were a suspect."

Kristen wiped a tear from her cheek and Dani walked over to her, lifting her chin. "That case is closed anyway as far as I know," she whispered.

Kristen closed her eyes, feeling the warmth of Dani's hand spread down her body.

"Do you want me to stay here tonight? Or you can come stay with me if you want." Dani wiped another tear as it escaped Kristen's brown eyes.

"I need to clean this place up, but I'd definitely feel safer if you stayed here with me."

"Alright. I'm going to tell Wilbur he can go. I'll be right back."

After the young deputy drove away, Dani walked around the house to the dock. Thousands of stars filled the darkened sky, and the light of the full moon cast a beautiful glow across the lake, shimmering on the surface of the crystal-clear water. She wondered if Kristen was telling the truth. The thought of someone trying to hurt her made Dani's blood pressure rise.

"Is everything okay?" Kristen asked, walking up behind her. "I thought maybe you'd left."

"I'm fine, just thinking."

Kristen stepped up next to her. "Do you remember diving off the end of this dock and trying to catch the fish with our bare hands?"

Dani laughed. "Yeah. We were a mess back then."

Kristen chuckled. "We sure had a lot of fun together, right here in this very spot."

"It's the first place you kissed me," Dani said, turning to face her.

"I remember that. It was your birthday, and you spent the night with us. We were trying to feed the fish animal crackers, and I kissed your cheek."

Dani smiled. "We were so innocent and naïve at that age, but I knew in that moment something was different."

"Me too."

Dani wrapped her arms around Kristen, pulling her close. Kristen threaded her arms around Dani's waist and laid her head on her shoulder. They stood at the end of the dock, holding each other in the moonlight, until a barking dog in the distance grabbed their attention. Dani couldn't remember the last time she'd simply held another woman and having Kristen back in her arms was almost too much to bear. Her body felt scorched from the heat of their embrace.

Kristen took a step back. She was afraid to look up at the smoldering eyes staring back at her. She wasn't sure she wanted to see what was in them. It would be so easy to fall in love with Dani all over again. She was past the point of having a torrid affair with her first love and she knew playing with the fire burning just below the surface between them was a bad idea. She was afraid once that fire got started it would consume them both, burning them to the ground before they could ever put it out. Still, looking up at Dani with her green eyes sparkling in the moonlight made Kristen want her that much more. She took another step back, adding more space between them.

"You back up any further and you're going for a swim." Dani grinned.

Kristen laughed, realizing her feet were inches away from the edge of the dock. "I'm going to go start straightening up the house," she said.

"I'm going to move my cruiser into the driveway. I'll be inside in a minute to help you," Dani replied, following her up the dock.

*

Dani got into her SUV and started the engine. She typed a quick note into the computer for dispatch, letting them know the scene was secure and the suspect could possibly be driving a small, dark colored sedan. After that, she pulled into the driveway and cut the engine. She wasn't sure if spending the night with Kristen was the best idea, but she needed to make sure she was safe. She'd let her guard slip on the dock, pulling Kristen into her arms. *How can a mistake feel so damn good?*

"Chief Ricketts?"

Dani jerked her head, shaking the thoughts away as she turned to see who was calling her name.

"Mrs. Cranston?" Dani squinted to see the little old lady through the trees. She exhaled loudly as she walked over to her.

"Is something wrong with Kristen?"

"No, ma'am."

"What happened?" the nosy old lady questioned.

Dani rolled her eyes. "There was a break in, but everything's fine. Did you happen to see anyone around the house this evening?"

"No. In fact, Kristen hasn't been there since yesterday morning around nine. She never came home at all yesterday or last night."

"Are you sure?" Dani asked.

"Oh yeah, my little Daisy barks every time she comes and goes," she countered, referring to her miniature dachshund. "She barked earlier this evening, and I saw Kristen's car in her driveway. The next thing I know, you and the other deputy arrived with your lights and sirens."

"Alright, well make sure your windows and doors are all locked."

"Are you spending the night?"

"Yes. You know Kristen and I have been friends since we were kids. I just want to make sure whoever broke in doesn't come back. Have a good night, Mrs. Cranston," she said, walking back across the driveway.

Dani wondered where Kristen had been over the past twenty-four hours. She mentioned she had been out running errands but never made reference to being away from the house for nearly two days. Dani shoved her hands into the front pockets of her jeans and walked back into the house.

Kristen had changed into soft cotton shorts and an old t-shirt, with her hair pulled back in a loose ponytail. Dani leaned against the door frame, watching the trim muscles of her tan legs flex as she moved around, straightening out the random items strewn about the living room. Dani felt a familiar tingle in the pit of her gut as it slid lower.

It would be so easy to step up behind her and slide my hand up those shorts. She doesn't even know what she's offering, and I want it, damn it. Dani's mouth watered and her heart raced. She took a step forward, with her eyes blazing a trail over Kristen's body as all rational thought escaped through her ears.

Dani grunted loudly when Kristen bent over to pick up something she'd dropped. Hearing the noise, Kristen turned around.

"I didn't hear you come in," Kristen said. She raised an eyebrow as Dani peeled her eyes away and walked briskly past her, into the kitchen.

Lord, have mercy! That woman would make Jesus commit a sin. Dani shook her head, pouring herself a glass of ice water and drinking half of it in one long swallow. *God, I want her so damn badly, I'm liable to die of need before this night is over. Why the hell did I offer to stay?*

"Are you okay?" Kristen asked as she rearranged the plastic flowers from the vase that had been knocked over.

"If I die tonight, I want to be buried in the Cadillac of caskets, black and chrome with an off-white, satin interior," Dani muttered. *If I go up in flames, at least I'll be going out in style.*

"What?" Kristen asked, walking into the kitchen. "You're mumbling."

"Nothing," Dani replied, drinking her second glass of water as the fuzz in her mind began to clear.

"Are you hungry?"

You have no idea, Dani thought, squeezing her eyes shut. "Sure, I'll make a sandwich or something."

"A sandwich? really?"

"Why not?"

"Is that how you stay so lean? You look like you live in the gym," Kristen said, eyeing the muscular curves of Dani's forearms.

Looking at me like that is not helping! Dani contemplated pouring the iced water over her head but chose to step out of the kitchen instead. The crotch of her jeans was starting to chafe from the wet underwear between her legs.

"If you're cooking, I'll just have whatever you're making. That's fine with me." Dani moved back into the living room, picking up a stack of books that had been knocked off a shelf. "Do you want me to go straighten up the bedrooms?"

"I already finished upstairs. I did that when I went up to change. I couldn't stand looking at it. I haven't messed with the back bedroom down here, but it didn't look like much was touched in there though."

"I'll take a look," Dani announced as she walked down the hall.

She was standing in the bedroom, staring at the closed window that she'd found opened two hours ago. Something about the fact that nothing in the room was out of place didn't sit right with Dani. All the other rooms in the house were in some sort of disarray and if this room was the first room he'd entered, wouldn't he start looking here for whatever it was he was after? She thought about the neighbor saying that Kristen hadn't been home in almost two days. She took the cell phone from her pocket and pulled up the app for the local weather. She thought it had rained the night before. She scrolled back over the past forty-eight hours and saw that it had in fact rained. Putting the phone away, she felt the carpet next to the window. It was completely dry and didn't feel hard like it had previously been soaked by the rain.

"Dinner's ready," Kristen called from down the hall. "I made shrimp and vegetable stir fry. I hope that's okay," she said, stepping into the room.

"It's fine," Dani replied, standing up.

"What are you doing?"

"I was just feeling around to see if the intruder dropped anything, but the carpet's clean." *No water and no mud or dirt from the ground outside.* "I'm starving." Dani smiled, easing past her and walking back to the kitchen.

The dining room table was set with two steaming plates of food adjacent to each other with silverware, napkins, and two glasses of iced water. Dani washed her hands in the kitchen sink, drying them on the hand towel before taking a seat at the table.

The food tasted as delicious as it looked. Dani's stomach growled as she cleaned her plate.

"That was unbelievable."

"Thanks," Kristen smiled, shyly. She couldn't remember the last time she'd cooked dinner for someone.

Dani opened the notebook she had in her pocket. "What time did you say you were gone today? I forgot to write that down early," she lied.

"I was out most of the day running errands."

"What time did you leave?"

"I don't know. Why does that matter? I wasn't here, and then I came home to find my house turned upside down," Kristen huffed, taking their plates to the kitchen and loading them into the dishwater.

"Mrs. Cranston stopped me when I was moving my truck."

Kristen shook her head. "That woman is going to drive me crazy."

"She said you'd been gone since yesterday morning."

"What?"

"You never came home yesterday, didn't sleep here last night, and didn't return today until you found the house tossed."

"That's what she told you?"

"Why would you lie to me, Kristen?"

"You're seriously going to believe that old battle axe over me? I think I know where I was, Dani!" she snapped. "I'm glad to know she has nothing to do, except clock each time I come and go." She shook her head.

Dani rose from the table and met her in the kitchen. "Whether she's telling the truth or not, I'd hope for the sake of our friendship and what we've meant to each other most of our lives, you wouldn't lie to me."

"It doesn't matter if I was here last night or not. Someone still broke in."

"A window was open, the house was methodically rearranged, and nothing was taken, except for your gun."

"You sound like you don't believe me. Do you think I did this to my own house, Dani?"

Dani shrugged. "I didn't say anything. I'm merely stating the facts. I believe you, Kristen."

"Yeah, well accusing me left and right doesn't feel like it to me," Kristen sneered.

"I will always believe you over anyone else and if someone really is trying to hurt you, they'll have to come through me to do it."

Kristen ignored her, stepping out of the kitchen. "I'm going to bed. I've had enough excitement for one night. You can sleep in either spare room. It doesn't matter to me." She turned to walk up the stairs and stopped. "It's weird saying goodnight to you in my house."

"I'm sorry I upset you. The curiosity in me sometimes takes over rationality. That's what makes me great at my job, but most of the time it bites me in the ass with everything else."

Kristen smiled slightly. "I'm fine. I'm just tired and it's been a long day. I'll be able to sleep knowing you're here. Thank you for staying."

Dani watched her walk away, before turning out the lights and stretching out on the couch.

Chapter 12

Kristen awoke in a fit the next morning, as the sun began to rise over the lake. She was surprised she was up so early after waking up in the middle of the night and finding Dani asleep on the couch. She was still dressed in everything, but her sneakers. Kristen had covered her with a throw blanket, watched her sleep and listened to her mumble in her dreams, until she had been too tired to stay up any longer. She'd finally gone back to bed, where she'd tossed and turned for hours, dreaming of the slumbering woman on the couch, wrapped around her naked body, begging for release.

She jumped up, wondering if Dani was awake as she wrapped her robe around herself and padded down the stairs. The house was empty, and the throw blanket was neatly folded on the arm of the couch. *Damn it!*

Kristen ran a hand loosely through her hair. She'd never wanted someone so much in her life, while loathing them at the same time. Dani always had a wicked way of making her body beg to be touched without even knowing it. She pulled her robe tighter, shaking her head.

"A cold shower sounds like a great idea," she said aloud, turning to go back up the stairs. A loud knock on the French doors of the patio scared her, causing her to shriek.

Kristen could barely make out a silhouette of someone standing on the back patio, through the curtains. She bolted back up the stairs and peered out of the blinds on the French doors that led to the balcony off the master bedroom and over the patio. The white sheriff's office boat was tied to the end of her dock and Dani was walking back towards it. She flung the door open and rushed outside.

*

Dani was about to climb back onto the boat when she heard her name. She spun around to see Kristen on the upstairs balcony in her robe with her hands waving in the air. She smiled, walking back towards her.

"What the hell are you doing up so early?" Kristen chided.

"I'm usually on shift before the sun comes up every day."

"Where's your uniform?"

"It's my day off," Dani called back up to her.

"Then why aren't you sleeping?"

Dani laughed. "I'm going fishing. Do you want to go?"

"Fishing?"

"Yes. I stopped to see if maybe you were up. I'm sorry if I woke you."

"No, you didn't, I just got up a little bit ago. Why did you leave so early?"

"I had plans." Dani nodded towards the boat. "Come down here before Mrs. Cranston comes outside."

Kristen laughed and went back into the house. A minute later she opened the patio door.

"When did you start talking in your sleep?" Kristen asked, smiling as Dani's eyes ran over her robe covered figure.

Dani raised an eyebrow and shrugged. "I don't know. I wasn't aware of it. What did you do, sneak down here to watch me sleep?"

"No. I wanted some water, and I noticed you were on the couch. I told you to use one of the spare rooms."

"I used to wake up and find you watching me sleep, when I actually did get any sleep."

Kristen rolled her eyes.

"Anyway, I was fine. You must be behind the blanket that mysteriously appeared on me."

"Yeah, it was cool in the house, so I laid it over you. I wasn't expecting you to be gone when I woke up though."

"I have to go out early, otherwise Leroy Johnson steals my fishing spot."

Kristen laughed. "I can't believe he's still alive."

"Me either!"

"You and that old man have been fighting over the same fishing hole for twenty years. The lake is five miles long. There has to be more than one perfect spot."

Dani grinned. "There's only one spot with mangroves and huge fish living under them." She checked her watch. "I need to get moving. Do you want to come with me?"

"I haven't fished in twelve years."

"So, it's like riding a bike. You don't forget it."

Kristen didn't actually have plans for the day and spending time with Dani sounded nice, but she wasn't sure she could trust herself. Still, a day out on the water would probably do her some good. *It's not like we're going to throw down and get naked on the floor of the sheriff's office boat.* She grinned wickedly.

"What are you thinking about?" Dani asked, watching her face change.

"Huh? Oh, nothing. Give me a few minutes to throw some clothes on."

"Alright. I'll meet you on the boat. I have food, drinks, and sunscreen, so you don't need to bring anything."

"Okay."

"Make sure you lock the doors and windows."

"Yes, officer." Kristen smiled, shaking her head.

*

"I have a bite!" Kristen yelled.

Dani dropped her pole and moved to the front of the boat to help her. "Did you forget how to reel it in?" she teased.

"I told you it's been a long time," Kristen exclaimed, turning the crank on the reel and tugging back on the pole.

Dani peered over the side of the boat. "Oh, that's a nice one!" She reached for the line with a serious expression on her face, pulling like she'd hooked a trophy fish.

"Where is it? Let me see it!" Kristen laid the pole down, hurrying to see her catch.

Dani laughed hysterically as she revealed the tiny trout on the other end of the line.

"You ass!" Kristen yelled, smacking her in the arm.

"Ouch!" Dani grimaced, removing the hook from the little fish's mouth. "Do you want to give him a kiss?"

Kristen sat on the console seat with her arms crossed. She had one eyebrow raised and her lips were pursed in an angry expression.

Dani leaned over the side and delicately placed the fish back into the water.

"I don't get it. We've been out here for hours and you're catching fish after fish. I finally get one bite and it's a damn guppy," Kristen growled in frustration as she opened her water bottle.

Dani walked over and sat down next to her on the bench seat. "Fishing is all about finesse. At least you caught one."

"You're not helping." Kristen furrowed her eyebrows, taking a sip of water and staring at the woman next to her. She was glad they were both wearing sunglasses. She wasn't sure she could handle seeing the sultry green eyes she knew were staring back at her.

Kristen's lips were wet and inviting with a trickle of water running down her chin. Dani's stomach knotted and she swallowed the lump in her throat as she imagined licking the cool droplet from her skin. Her muscles tensed. She tingled from head to toe. Her pulse quickened as she closed the distance between them, pressing her lips to Kristen's.

The kiss was slow and welcoming. Dani ran her tongue over Kristen's soft lips, licking the last of the cold water from them before slipping inside her mouth. Kristen's breath hitched in her throat. She ran her hand over the top of Dani's chest near her collar bone as she kissed her back with every ounce of desire that had been building inside of her over the past two months.

They panted softly, kissing passionately like long lost lovers finding home again. Dani moved to pull Kristen into her lap.

Kristen pushed away from her. "There's a boat coming this way," she shrieked breathlessly.

Dani squinted her eyes to see who it was as she caught her breath and slowed her racing heart. "It's only Mr. Baumgartner."

"Our sophomore history teacher? He's still alive?" Kristen watched the boat moving past as the fuzziness in her head began to clear.

"Yeah."

"Do you think he saw us?"

Dani laughed. "Nah, he's blind as a bat. We actually revoked his license last year after he failed his driving test for the third time."

Kristen's eyebrows furled together. "You let him fail it three times!"

Dani shrugged. "I don't write the laws."

"How the hell is he allowed to drive a boat if he can't see to drive a car?"

"You don't need a license to drive a boat."

"Oh, good lord." Kristen shook her head.

Dani chuckled. "I better get you home. I promised to help my parents at the store this afternoon. My father redesigned the layout of the backroom and he's in over his head trying to get everything straightened out."

Kristen nodded. "How many employees do they have now?"

Dani thought for a second as she stowed their fishing equipment. "Oh, probably a dozen full and part-time combined."

"I remember working there as a stocker and a cashier when we were in high school. I always thought you'd be running that place one day."

Dani shook her head as she started the engine. "I found something that suited me a whole lot more, I guess. I'm sure they will leave it to me when they pass, but hopefully it runs itself by then."

"I'm surprised none of the larger chains have come to town."

"They've tried, but Cypress Lake is small. We only have about a thousand people here. Piggly Wiggly and

Walmart don't fit demographics like ours." Dani spoke loud enough to be heard over the outboard motor.

Kristen nodded. She'd pushed the heated kiss they'd shared to the back of her mind, but she didn't think her scorched lips were ever going to let her forget it.

Dani pulled up at the dock and idled the engine.

"When will I see you again?" Kristen asked as she climbed out.

"I'm not sure. I'm back on shift tomorrow for the next five days." She grinned, leaning on the handrail of the center console and pushing her sunglasses up on her head. She knew she was playing with fire and liable to get burned, but she was powerless when it came to this woman. Kristen had come back into her life, knocking down the walls that she had carefully constructed around her heart.

Kristen shook her head, smiling the cutest come-hither smile that Dani had ever seen. "Whenever you get some free time, you know where to find me," she answered over her shoulder as she walked up the dock.

Dani Ricketts was sexy as hell and the sinful look in her wild green eyes had always driven Kristen out of her mind. She was almost too far gone to remember why she was in town to begin with.

Dani's knees felt weak, watching Kristen's ass move under her shorts as she walked away. She thought about jumping out and running after her, but she wasn't sure she could find the separation between casual sex and making love, at least not where Kristen was concerned and she still had no idea how long she was in town, or even why she had returned.

"Maybe I should just stick my damn head in that cooler full of melted ice," she muttered to herself as she drove off.

Chapter 13

Two weeks later, Dani was sitting in Sheriff Fisher's office, popping green grapes into her mouth as he read the Mayor's statement out loud. Roger Fillmore's toxicology report had come back the week before with marijuana in his system. Consequently, he and Paul Davis's homicide cases were being blamed on a drug gang in the city and thus closed by the mayor himself.

"It sounds like he wrapped this problem up with a pretty little bow and pink ribbon just in time for the election," she said, tossing another grape into her mouth.

"Yeah, oh well, it's out of our hands now. You're eating those nasty things like they're candy," he grimaced.

Dani laughed. "It wouldn't hurt you to eat something healthy every now and then," she replied, chucking one at him. It bounced off, rolling on the floor back towards her.

"You better pick that up before we get ants in here!"

She shook her head. "Ants don't appear in seconds."

"They probably won't eat it anyway. Yuck."

"What's wrong with grapes?"

"They're gross."

Dani rolled her eyes. "Let me guess, pretzels and cheese doodles are your preferred snacks."

Sheriff Fisher chewed the corner of his white mustache. "You think you know everything don't you? I do believe there's a criminal justice degree in your file, not a medical one."

Dani shrugged. "Suit yourself."

He watched her get up and move towards the door. "Don't forget your droppings," he grumbled.

She rolled her eyes, picking the grape up from the floor and throwing it into his trash can. She walked out of his office, but stuck her head back in. "Wilbur just signed on. I'm gone."

"Have a good night," he called back.

*

Dani had thought about stopping by Kristen's but drove straight home instead. She hadn't seen her since she'd dropped her off on the dock. She'd picked up the phone to call her half a dozen times, but she wasn't sure what to say. She knew what would happen when she saw her again and she wasn't sure if she was ready to cross that line. Of course, her body was ready. In fact, it was more than willing. The memory of her broken heart was the one thing that was holding her back. She wasn't sure how long Kristen was in town, but eventually she'd be gone again, and Dani would be left to pick up the shattered pieces one more time.

She changed from her uniform to running shorts and a t-shirt and opened a beer as she turned the TV on. A knock on her door made the hair on the back of her neck stand up. She checked the peephole before going for her gun and backed away smiling.

"Hey, Mom," she said, opening the door and hugging her. "Where's Dad?"

"In the office. We're about to leave for the day," she replied, handing her a brown sack.

"What's this?" Dani asked, closing the door.

Her mother walked over to pet the skinny orange cat standing on the edge of the kitchen table, stretching as far as he could to get scratched on the head.

"Candles. Barbara Klein started selling them for some catalog company. I bought a bunch of them and thought you might like a few. I forgot to give them to you the other day."

Dani pulled the three glass jars from the bag, sniffing them one at a time. The first one was called Thunderstorm and smelled like laundry soap and salt. Dani shrugged, setting it on the table. The next was called Willow Branch and smelled like old trees and ginger. The last one smelled like flowers and lemon. She turned it over to read the name on the bottom. It was called Sunshine. She opened the top and smelled it again. The enchanting scent reminded her of Kristen.

"I can't believe a good boy like you has a such a horrible name," her mother said to the cat as she scratched him under his chin and rubbed his head between his ears.

"What's wrong with his name?" Dani questioned as she walked across the room, setting the Sunshine candle on the nightstand next to her bed.

"Really, Dani? Who names their pet, Asshole Cat?" she chided, raising an eyebrow.

Dani laughed. "His name's Cat. I just call him asshole."

"He still deserves a proper name and what's so bad about him anyway?"

"Let's see … he clawed holes in my uniform pants, shit in my favorite shoes, tore up the window blinds … twice … oh and he's clawed and bitten me more times than I care to count."

Her mother shook her head. "Well, you found a stray feral kitten and decided to keep him. What did you expect? He looks fine to me." She rubbed his back.

"I'll trade you the cat for the candles ... even the Willow Branch one," Dani exclaimed, wrinkling her nose.

"I bought them for you, silly. If you don't like them, give them to the sheriff."

"Fine, take him home with you then."

"Yeah right, like you would part with this cat," she laughed.

Dani went back to the couch and her beer as another knock sounded at the door. She sighed and got up to open it.

"Hey, Dad," she said, hugging him.

"She's trying to give me her cat," her mother said.

Her father laughed, shaking his head as he walked over to his wife. "They have a love/hate relationship. That cat loves to piss her off and she pretends to hate him. That's why I see her buying him treats all the time." He scratched the animal on the top of his head and the cat stretched like it was the greatest thing in the world to be petted by people.

Dani rolled her eyes at the display show the cat was putting on for her parents.

"Do you have another one of those?" her father asked, nodding towards the beer she was sipping.

"In the fridge," Dani replied.

"You know the damndest thing," her mother blurted, sitting down next to Dani on the couch. "I swear I saw Kristen Malone in the store the other day. She must have a cousin or something that still lives here."

"No, it was her. She's back in town."

"Really? Since when?"

"I don't know ... two months I guess."

"So, you've seen her then?"

"Yeah, a few times. Paul Davis's body was found at her dock."

"Are you serious? I knew he was found in the lake, but the paper didn't say exactly where. That's a little strange, isn't it?"

Dani shrugged. "The case was officially closed today, so I don't really care where he was found."

"What did she say when she saw you?"

"Not much, Mom. I think she was surprised that I'd become a deputy, but I was there on business, so we didn't stroll down memory lane. I don't think she wants anyone to know she's in town."

"What made her come back?"

Dani shrugged, sipping the last of her beer. "She's selling her parent's house or something. Like I said, we haven't talked much."

"So, she didn't say why she left so abruptly?"

"Nope. It's all in the past, where it belongs."

Dani knew her mother was only trying to help. It hadn't been easy for her to watch her daughter mope around with a broken heart. She'd known the two young girls were in love and although it had been different than what she knew, she'd never thought of doing anything to take the happiness away from her daughter or wipe the huge smile off her face. The light in Dani's eyes had burned out when Kristen left Cypress Lake without a word and never returned.

Her mother patted her on the leg. "Well, you're a grown woman and I trust you to make your own decisions." She stood up and walked over to the door with her husband. "Take her a candle." She smiled sheepishly.

Dani laughed and shook her head, locking the door behind them as they left.

*

The next afternoon, Dani was driving around the access roads to the lake and decided to stop when she saw Kristen's car in her driveway. Pulling her SUV off the road at the end of her driveway, she cut the engine and grabbed the brown sack from the passenger seat.

Kristen pulled the door open and leaned against the frame. She held back her excitement at seeing the other woman in her uniform. She wasn't sure what it was. Unlike most lesbians, women in uniform didn't do it for her, but Dani was sexy as hell in her sheriff's uniform. Her mind drifted towards racy thoughts of stripping her out of it, one layer at a time.

Kristen's big brown eyes sparkled in the sun. She was dressed in cut-off jean shorts and a white tank top. Her wavy hair was pulled back in a clip with her bangs brushed to the side of her forehead. She looked young, reminding Dani of the girl she used to love. The adorable smile on her face tugged at Dani's heart.

"I was beginning to think you'd forgotten where I lived," Kristen exclaimed.

Dani ached to touch her but shoved the brown bag at her instead.

"What's this?"

"Candles," Dani replied.

Kristen peered inside the bag. "I don't see or hear from you in over two weeks, and you bring me a candle. What the hell?"

Dani shrugged, placing her hands on the utility belt of her uniform. "My mom says hi, by the way."

"How does she know I'm here?"

"She saw you at their store."

"Damn."

"Those are from her. Well, technically, she brought me three of them and I kept one. I figured you might want the others. I'll take them back to my house if you don't want them."

"What girl doesn't like candles?" Kristen scolded. "What I don't understand, is why it took you so long to see me again."

"I've been busy tying up the loose ends of that homicide investigation, so the mayor could close it in time to start his re-election campaign, without the negative impact of the unsolved case on his back."

Kristen raised an eyebrow. "That sounds rehearsed," she said, pulling the tops off the candle jars.

"No, it's more like the truth. I almost wish another dead body would show up just to put a wrench in his happy little plans. He's such a dickhead."

Kristen laughed, sniffing the candles. She pushed the lid back down on the first and reached for the second. "Oh … this one smells like you."

"Which one?" Dani asked, grabbing it from her. The word Thunderstorm was written on the bottom of the jar. "This one stinks."

"No, it doesn't. It smells like you and I'm going to put it in my room."

Dani rolled her eyes, purposely avoiding the fact that she'd done the same thing with the Sunshine candle. She was about to reply with some flirtatious remark when the radio crackled on her hip. She turned the volume up, listening to the report from one of her deputies who was stopping a suspicious dark car.

"Do you think that's—"

Kristen was cut off when the call for assistance came across the radio. Dani quickly grabbed the microphone attached to the shoulder board of her shirt and pressed the button.

"Dispatch, this is Chief Ricketts. I'm 10-76 to Sandbar Road. Copy?" she said, rushing out of the house. "I'm about to find out," she yelled back to Kristen as she ran to her SUV.

Kristen watched as Dani made a U-turn out of her driveway and roared down the road with her lights flashing and siren wailing. She silently prayed for her safety as she closed the door, drowning out the high-pitched noise in the distance.

Chapter 14

Dani raced down Lake Drive, skidding around the corner on her way to the distress call as the radio in her SUV buzzed.

"Dispatch, be advised, I'm 10-80, heading northbound on Sandbar Road. Copy?" Wilbur said.

Dani shook her head. The driver of the suspicious car had obviously taken off and now he was in pursuit of the vehicle. She grabbed the microphone on the side of her computer.

"Wilbur, Chief Ricketts, I'm 10-76. Copy?"

"Copy, Chief."

"I'm going to go down Main and try to cut him off at Cedar Avenue. Keep me posted on your twenty. Copy?" She floored the gas and turned her headlights on as she turned onto Main Street. The sun was going down rapidly, and they would be under the cover of darkness within minutes.

"Roger," he replied.

"Dispatch, Chief Ricketts, advise all 10-86. Copy?"

"Roger, Chief," the deputy running dispatch answered as he sent out an updated email about the pursuit, including the current location and vehicle description, across their computer system to all deputies that were on shift.

"Chief, turning west on Pine Lane," Wilbur radioed.

"Roger, I just crossed Main and Palm." She pressed the gas pedal to the floor as she displayed a mental map of the town streets in her head. The suspect was obviously trying to get out of town. There were only three roads that actually led out of town, and she hoped he chose the one that she was on.

"Chief, what's your twenty?" Wilbur asked frantically.

"I'm turning onto Cedar from Main," she answered.

"He turned his lights off. He should be heading in your direction."

"Damn it." She shook her head. The sun was long gone, and the roads were pitch black at night on the edge of town. She turned her high beams on, scanning the road in front of her for the dark car.

"I've lost visual. Copy?" Wilbur radioed.

"Roger—" she let go of the microphone button as something raced past her in the oncoming lane. She smashed the brakes, skidding to a stop as she cut a U-turn in the middle of the road and floored the gas pedal once again. "Dispatch, be advised, vehicle is rolling dark and headed east on Cedar Avenue at approximately eighty to one hundred miles per hour," she radioed as Wilbur's lights appeared in her rearview mirror.

They chased the shadow through the darkness until they reached Main Street and quickly turned north, following the road until they were outside of the town limits. The car was nowhere around and had obviously made it out of town.

"Son of a bitch!" Dani yelled, smacking her hand on the steering wheel.

There was nothing except woods on the two lane road for the next twenty miles. She slowed down and pulled off the road on the shoulder. Wilbur pulled over behind her and got out of his cruiser.

"Damn it," he said, shaking his head.

"He's long gone by now," she sighed. "Did you get a good look at the vehicle?"

"Yeah. It was a dark gray, two-door Nissan, and maybe four or five years old."

"Did you get the plate?"

"It had some kind of dark cover over the plate, which is why I stopped him to begin with. I couldn't read the digits."

"Fuck!" Dani shook her head. "Did you get a look at him before he drove off?"

"Not really. His window was down when I got out of my cruiser, and I could see a white male in a black ball cap in the side mirror. His face was scruffy, like he hadn't shaved in a few days. He rolled the window up and floored the gas when I reached his rear tire."

"Alright. Head back to the station and write up a report. Make sure you give it to dispatch so they can send out a fresh BOLO alert."

"Yes, ma'am."

*

Dani headed towards her apartment but turned down a side road at the last minute, leading towards the lake. She wasn't sure what she was doing as she turned down Lake Drive and pulled into a driveway. Her mind was racing in different directions. She had no idea who was in the car, or even if it was the person that Kristen had seen following her. Either way, it was suspicious enough for her to worry about Kristen's safety.

Dani knocked on the door and rested her hands on her utility belt. She was starting to get tired as she came down from the natural adrenaline rush of the endless pursuit.

Kristen opened the door, slightly surprised to see her. "Did you catch him?" she asked.

"No." Dani shook her head, walking inside. "Whoever he is, he knows what he is doing. He's a white guy, in need of a shave and wears a dark ball cap."

Kristen smirked. "That could be most of the guys in this town."

"Yeah, I know. He was driving a dark gray, two-door Nissan."

Kristen blew out a frustrating breath. "Sounds a lot like the car that's been following me."

"I tried to catch him, but the asshole turned his lights out. He knew exactly where he was and where he was headed. I bet he was going every bit of a hundred miles an hour."

"Wow."

"I was so close, but he blew past me like a shadow."

"That's how he keeps appearing behind me, like a shadow that's following me. He's never close enough for me to see him or get a good look at his car, and then he vanishes. It makes me even more nervous now. If this was the same person, what the hell does he want with me? I'm starting to think someone is after me, Dani."

"I won't let anyone hurt you. I promise," Dani said, wrapping her arms around Kristen. She inhaled the scent of her shampoo mixed with light perfume. It swirled around her mind, igniting all her senses.

Dani pulled her head back, meeting Kristen's eyes before kissing her softly. Kristen ran her hands up the front of Dani's uniform, over her breasts, to the soft skin at the back of her neck below her ponytail. The kiss was gentle and probing at first but heated quickly. Dani pulled Kristen tightly against her as their bodies molded into one.

The radio on Dani's hip crackled, separating them like a bolt of electricity. Kristen put her hand to her lips. The taste of Dani's mouth still lingered on them.

"I'm sorry. I didn't mean—"

"Dani, we have a lot of history, and the attraction is obviously still very strong between us. Don't be sorry for something we both wanted," Kristen said.

"I should go," Dani replied, backing up towards the door. "Let me know if you see that car again and make sure you keep your doors and windows locked. I'll put an extra patrol on your house if you want me to."

"No. There's no need to do that. I'll be fine."

"Okay ... well, goodnight then."

"Goodnight," Kristen whispered, watching Dani walk down the driveway. Her body tingled and it took everything she had not to run after her.

*

Dani walked into her apartment and peeled out of her uniform. She poured a glass of whiskey from the bottle she kept on the top of the fridge, drinking half of it before changing into shorts and a t-shirt. Nothing on the TV kept her attention as she flipped from channel to channel. She wasn't hungry and didn't feel like showering. Her mind kept replaying the kiss that clung to her lips.

Dani finally gave up on clearing her head and went to bed. She tossed and turned for an hour, restlessly thinking about the look in Kristen's eyes, the softness of her lips and the way her body had felt against her. Dani fought her inner self. Fanning the flames of the fire burning between them wasn't a good idea and deep down she knew that, but the more she tried to rationalize her thoughts, the more she wanted Kristen.

Desire finally won the battle. Dani tore the sheet to the side and shot out of her bed like she was on speed. Dressing quickly in jeans and a t-shirt, she snatched her phone and keys from the nightstand and tripped over the cat as she raced towards the door.

*

Kristen was getting ready for bed when she heard pounding on the door. Scared, she reached for her gun, cursing silently when she remembered it had been stolen. She crossed the hall to the front bedroom and peered through the blinds at the sheriff's office SUV parked in her driveway.

She rushed down the stairs in a t-shirt and shorts with nothing under them and squinted to look through the peephole at the woman on the doorstep. Dani was standing under the moonlight in jeans and white t-shirt. Her hair was down, grazing the top of her shoulder on one side and tucked behind her ear on the other.

Kristen turned the lock and pulled the door open. "Dani?" she questioned.

Dani walked inside, wrapped her arms around Kristen and kissed her deeply. The shock of seeing Dani at her door wore off quickly and she shoved it closed. Dani spun her around, backing her up against the wall as she kissed her passionately, pushing her thigh between Kristen's legs and drinking from the mouth she so desperately craved.

Kristen moved involuntarily against the body pressing her to the wall. She throbbed between her legs, feeling the warm wetness soak her shorts as she ran her hands through

Dani's hair. She felt like she'd internally combust from the pressure building inside. She'd never wanted anything so badly in all her life. She reached down, pulling Dani's shirt, frantically trying to get it off her.

Dani backed away, pulling her shirt over her head and pushed back against Kristen in one fluid motion. Kristen's mouth watered as she ran her hands over the lithe muscles and subtle curves of Dani's upper body.

Clothes were traded for skin on skin as Dani pulled Kristen off the wall. They fumbled around blindly, never letting go of one another, landing on the couch with Dani on top, gasping and kissing wildly. Kristen wrapped her legs around Dani's, thrusting up into her with each pass of her tongue.

Dani worked her hand between them and down to the wetness that was coating her stomach. She circled Kristen's clit with her fingers, teasing her entrance as she tore her lips from Kristen's, kissing her neck before licking her nipples.

Kristen arched her back, moaning from pure pleasure as Dani's fingers eased inside of her. She saw the storm brewing in Dani's green eyes as she moved lower. Hanging halfway off the couch, she pressed her tongue to Kristen's pulsing clit, licking in circles as her fingers slid in deep, before pulling almost all the way out, and then back in again.

"Oh my God!" Kristen panted, squeezing her eyes shut and throwing her head back. She felt like she was flying a thousand miles an hour through the night sky on sensory overload. Kristen opened her eyes to see Dani looking back at her with the hungry eyes of a caged animal. She bit her bottom lip and ran her hand through Dani's hair, tugging her back up.

Their mouths met recklessly as Dani continued thrusting. Dani ignored the ache in her chest and the fire burning deep in her belly, losing herself in the feeling of Kristen's hot core wrapped around her fingers as she moved in and out of her.

The taste of herself on Dani's tongue overwhelmed her already heightened senses, causing an explosion deep inside of her as she came fiercely, gasping and jerking. She nearly flung Dani to the floor as her body released the weeks of pent-up lust that had been eating away at her.

Dani pulled her hand free, kissing Kristen's neck gently as she caught her breath. She grinned softly when dilated chocolate brown eyes met hers.

"I couldn't take it anymore," she whispered.

"I know." Kristen kissed her swollen lips. "Me, either."

Dani made a move to get up and Kristen grabbed her. "This isn't over." She smiled.

*

Dani awoke in the middle of the night in a strange bed. Realizing someone was next to her, she opened her eyes to see Kristen sound asleep. The memory of their lovemaking overwhelmed her. She pulled the covers off her nude body and walked over to the French doors that led to the balcony. The open curtains allowed the light in from the full moon glistening across the still water of the lake.

She looked back at the slumbering woman in the bed. Her hair cascaded across the top of her shoulders, spilling onto the pillow behind her head and her naturally tanned skin contrasted against the crisp white bedding. It was the most beautiful sight Dani had ever seen. A tear escaped her eye as she thought about the happiest night of her life, potentially being the biggest mistake of her life. She wiped the tear away and turned back towards the shiny lake.

A warm hand on her back made Dani's heart race. She melted into the body behind her. Kristen stepped closer, pressing herself to Dani's ass while running her hands over the front of her body. She skimmed her hands across the muscles of her flat stomach to her breasts, caressing each of them and teasing her nipples with her fingers and thumbs.

Dani watched as Kristen moved around her, running her hands over Dani's stomach as she pushed her against the door. Their mouths met tenderly at first, each taking what the other was giving. Kristen dropped her hand to Dani's thighs, rubbing her legs in lazy strokes while teasingly skimming across her center.

Dani's body tightened in anticipation. She ran her hands over Kristen's back and down to her ass, squeezing gently as their kiss deepened. When Kristen finally parted Dani's legs, sliding her fingers back and forth through her wetness, the blood in Dani's head rushed south, causing her to sway slightly from the dizziness. Kristen pressed her tightly against the wall, rubbing her harder and faster, before slipping inside of her.

Dani's body jerked as Kristen filled her. The smell of Kristen's shampoo mixed with her light perfume and the heady scent of sex in the air was intoxicating. Dani was lost in her own swirling arousal, kissing Kristen as if her life depended on it, while rocking her hips up and down on the fingers driving in and out of her.

Kristen pulled away from the kiss, trailing her mouth over Dani's upper body as she sank to her knees. The cool air stung the heated skin of Dani's exposed torso. She watched as Kristen spread her legs, snaking her tongue out and licking her slowly, stroke after stroke.

119

Dani's legs quivered. She could barely stand as Kristen put her lips on her, alternating sucking and licking her. She held Dani's hips against the French doors squishing her ass against the glass as she finished her with her mouth. Dani moaned and gasped when the orgasm tore through her. She jerked back, smacking her head on the glass behind her.

Kristen licked her way back up Dani's body to her mouth. Dani's muscles felt like mush around her bones, but she mustered the last of her energy and found the strength to pick Kristen up against her. She raised her eyebrows in surprise and wrapped her legs around Dani's waist as she walked them back to the bed.

Chapter 15

A week and half had gone by without Dani seeing Kristen again and Kristen hadn't exactly tried to see her either. She knew it had been a mistake before it had even happened. She'd gone to Kristen in the night knowing she was giving into the sinful desire that was driving her mad. She was willing to accept the broken heart that was bound to come with the night of unbridled passion, but she was still trying to avoid it, nonetheless. Staying away from Kristen was the easiest and hardest thing she'd ever had to do.

Dani threw herself headlong into her job, trying to keep her thoughts from wandering back to Kristen, but nothing could peel the image of her naked, yearning body off Dani's mind. She feared the picture was burned into her memory and would become a permanent fixture in her thoughts.

Dani walked into the station, tossed a brown paper sack onto her desk and walked to the vending machine at the end of the hall. She deposited the loose change from her pocket and pressed the button for water. Nothing happened. She pressed the button again and waited. The machine didn't make a sound.

"Damn piece of shit!" she growled, smacking the side of it. Finally, she shook her head and turned around to go back to her office.

"Everything okay?" Sheriff Fisher asked. He was standing a few feet away with his arms crossed and the key to the machine dangling from his hand.

"Peachy," she sneered, snatching the key from him to retrieve her drink.

"You've been on edge recently, Ricketts. Is something going on?"

She wasn't in the mood for twenty questions. All she wanted to do was sit down and eat her lunch in peace. This was the reason she'd chosen to eat lunch in her office, instead of the deli down the road where she'd purchased her sandwich.

"I'm fine," she said, handing him the key. "I haven't been sleeping well. I think I need a new bed or something," she lied.

"It could be the food you eat. Maybe your body is finally telling you that you need a cheeseburger," he called to her back as she walked down the hall.

"I had a pork sandwich yesterday at Smokey's," she yelled back.

"That place gave me the shits the last time I ate there," he grimaced. "Hey, maybe that's what's wrong with you."

Dani stuck her head out of her office and tossed a cherry tomato at him.

"You better pick that up!"

She laughed, ignoring him as she sat down at her desk to eat her turkey sandwich and side salad. What he didn't know was she'd also purchased a tiny slice of carrot cake for dessert. She devoured her food as she worked on the schedule for the following month. She liked to stay at least three weeks ahead and with the summer fast approaching, she needed to make sure each shift was double covered with an extra person patrolling on the lake. Many of the houses along the backside of the lake were rented out over the summer months. This brought extra traffic into town, on the streets, and on the water. The touristy time of year brought a lot of money to the town, so she couldn't complain, and it had always made her job interesting.

Dani balled up her trash and tossed it in the waste basket as she closed the screen on her computer. She was about to go back on patrol when she heard yelling down the hall. A call had just come across the radio, but she still had the volume turned down from her lunch break.

"Son of a bitch!" Sheriff Fisher shouted.

Dani stepped out of her office. "What's going on?"

"Pat Weaver just called. He found the handyman who's been doing some work on his lake house. This is not what we need right now."

Dani raised an eyebrow. "Okay? Found him where? Was he missing?"

"Found him dead!" he growled, pacing the floor. "The damn side of his head was bashed in."

"Oh shit."

"The mayor's going to have a field day with this!"

"Who is on scene?"

"Vince should be there in a minute. He was the closest to the area. Also, I think Henry's already been called too."

"Pat Weaver's house—"

"Oak Lane."

Dani nodded. She knew where the Weaver's house was located. She grabbed the radio attached to her shoulder as she headed out of the building. "Vince? Chief Ricketts, copy?"

"Roger, Chief."

"I'm 10-76, ETA five minutes. Secure the scene and don't touch anything," she said.

"Roger."

Dani squealed the tires as she floored the gas pedal coming out of the sheriff's office parking lot with the lights flashing and siren blaring on her SUV. She pulled off the side of the road behind Vince's cruiser and cut the engine. A line of yellow police tape circled the small house. She grabbed a pair of gloves from the back of her vehicle and ducked under the tape.

"Hey, Chief, you might want a mask. The smell is pretty bad," Vince uttered, wrinkling his nose.

"Great." She shook her head, walking through the front door behind him.

They walked through the living room to the kitchen. Dani held her hand over her nose to cover the rancid stench that smelled like rotting meat. The body was swollen and greenish blue in color and his skin looked sort of waxy, like he was fake and out of a Hollywood movie. He was slumped on his right side near the open cabinet doors under the sink where he'd obviously been working. Various tools were strung about beside him, as well as inside the cabinet. Dani stepped a little closer. The left side of the man's head was smashed in over his eye, as well as above his ear.

"Damn," she whispered, pulling her phone from her pocket. She took a couple dozen pictures of the body and the crime scene. She examined the man's tools for evidence, but everything was clean. "The killer must have taken the weapon with him. It's definitely none of these."

She pulled the notepad from her pocket, making notes as she went over the scene. From the position of the body, it looked like the man had been on his knees, working on the pipes under the sink. He probably turned around when someone walked up on him and that's when he was struck in the head.

"The owner called this in, correct?"

"Yes, ma'am. He's outside."

Dani followed Vince back outside where he pointed out the owner of the house. She took a few deep breaths of fresh air as she watched Henry park his white van in the driveway. "I'm going to talk to the owner. Go update Henry. I'll be inside in a minute," she said, walking towards the group of people standing next to the yellow tape line. "Patrick Weaver?"

"That's me," an older gentleman replied, stepping under the tape.

Dani walked him away from the group. "I need to ask you some questions. Firstly, do you know the man inside?"

"Yes. He's a handyman I hired to do some work on our rental house. His name is Larry Hicks."

Dani raised an eyebrow as she wrote the name on her notepad. Larry Hicks had been another classmate of her and Kirsten's. "When's the last time you talked to him?"

"I'd been trying to get a hold of him for about two weeks, I guess. That's why I finally drove up to see what was going on. My wife and I live in the city."

"Did he have anyone working with him?"

"No. At least, not that I know of."

"How long had he been working on your house?"

"Oh, about a month, maybe a little longer. We had him fix some rotten wood and do a few other odd jobs like painting and putting in a new garbage disposal."

"Was the front door closed and locked when you arrived?"

The man pursed his eyebrows in thought. "It was closed, but no, it wasn't locked. I turned the knob and walked right in."

"Alright. In a few minutes, I'll need you to go inside with one of my deputies and take a look around to see if anything is missing." She wrote a few more notes and walked over to the deputy cruiser pulling up alongside the curb.

"Chief." Wilbur nodded.

"Get your print kit and dust the front door."

"Yes, ma'am."

"When you're done," she nodded towards Mr. Weaver. "Take the owner around to see if anything was stolen. Wait for Henry to remove the body first though."

Dani walked the perimeter of the house, checking for signs of forced entry or exit before going back inside. Henry was kneeling next to the body.

"I'm starting to feel like a character in a crime novel," he said, looking back over his shoulder at her.

"Me too," she sighed.

"He's been here a while. I'd say ten days, two weeks at most, based on his level of decomposition and the temperature in here."

Dani's stomach rolled from the putrid smell and grotesque sight of the rotting body. "Any idea what he was hit with?"

"Nope. It was quick though. I'll know more once I get him on the table," he replied, walking past her to retrieve the stretcher from the van.

"Stay here and help Henry load him up. Then, I want you to question all the neighbors. See if they've seen anyone here with him," Dani said to Vince before walking away. She met Henry at the front door. "Call me the minute you have something."

"You got it," he replied, pushing the black gurney past her.

*

Dani walked into Sheriff's Fisher's office and pushed the door closed.

"I've been on the phone for the past hour with the mayor. How bad is it?"

"There's no sign of forced entry and the front door was unlocked. We were able to get a few prints from the handle, but more than likely they're the victim's. Henry said he was probably there about ten days."

"Do we know who he is?"

"Yeah, he's the hired handyman, Larry Hicks. He also happens to be another one of my high school classmates."

"Oh, that's fucking great! Are you telling me this is linked to the others?" He pursed his lips and shook his head.

"I don't know. His head was smashed in pretty good. It looked like a sneak attack. None of these homicides are the same. Larry, Roger, and Paul were all friends in school. I know Larry worked as a handyman doing odd jobs for people all over town. He could have still hung around them. I have no idea." She shrugged.

"Either we have one pissed off drug cartel, or a crazed serial killer who has pulled the wool over all our eyes. Any way you look at it, this isn't good," he sighed.

"I'm going to go talk to Roger's ex-wife and try to establish a connection," Dani replied.

"Three murders in two months. What the hell is going on in this town?"

"No idea." She shrugged.

"Let me know when you hear from Henry," he called to her back as she left the room.

Dani looked up the last known address for Larry Hicks before leaving the office. She drove towards the north edge of the town limit and pulled up in front of a small white house with a little red car in the driveway. She climbed out of the SUV and walked up to the front door, knocking a few times before settling her hands on her utility belt.

After a minute passed, Dani knocked again, harder this time. She tried the knob, but it was locked. She finally tapped her steel-toed boot against the bottom of the door.

"Sheriff's office," she shouted.

Dani was about to walk away when the door finally opened. A redheaded woman answered in a semi disordered state. She looked like she'd been either passed out in the middle of the afternoon or strung out on drugs.

"Ma'am, do you know a man named Larry Hicks?"

"Yes, he's my roommate," she yawned.

Dani's ears perked up. "When's the last time that you saw him?"

"I don't know. I work the nightshift out at the truck stop by the highway. I don't see Larry very much."

"I really need you to think about the last time that you saw him," Dani stressed.

The woman ran a hand through her shaggy hair. "I guess it's been about two weeks. I went to see my cousin in the city, so I was gone for a few days, and I don't remember seeing him since I've been back. Why? What did he do?"

"What's your name?" Dani asked.

"Darlene Hill."

Dani wrote her name in the notepad she was holding. "Larry was found dead this morning."

"Oh my God!" Darlene exclaimed, covering her mouth with her hands.

"Did he owe anyone money? Have any enemies?"

"No. I don't think so, but like I said, I didn't see him often."

"How long did he live here?"

"Oh, about eight or ten months. I lost my second job and took a roommate to help pay the bills."

"I need to take a look at his room. Will that be okay?"

"Yeah, sure. How did … What happened?" Darlene asked, showing Dani to his room.

"I can't give you the details. All I can say is … someone killed him."

"Oh God," Darlene gasped.

Dani pulled a pair of gloves from her pocket and searched the drawers of his room. She found a few receipts and job estimates, and a few rolled up marijuana joints, but nothing else.

"I told him no drugs in the house after I caught him smoking pot when he first moved in," Darlene shrieked. "He swore he wouldn't bring it back." She shook her head, watching Dani walk outside.

Dani grabbed an evidence bag from her SUV and returned to the room, stuffing the drugs inside.

"Ms. Hill, do you know Roger Fillmore or Paul Davis?"

"No."

Dani pulled her phone from her pocket and scrolled to find the pictures of the two men. "What about these two guys?" she asked.

"Yeah, I saw them a few times when Larry first moved in, but I haven't seen them in months. Like I said, I work the graveyard shift, and I pick up double shifts a lot of the time. I rarely saw Larry."

"Okay." Dani took a picture of a framed photo of Larry with another guy that looked like it was maybe his father. She cropped the picture and blew it up before saving it on her phone. "One more question. Do you know if he has any family in town?"

"He never spoke about his family. I think he mentioned his father died, but other than that, no."

"Alright. Here's my card. Call me if you think of anything."

"Should I be worried? I mean, if someone killed him … do you think they will come after me? I barely knew the man. If he was in trouble …"

"Keep your doors and windows locked and you should be fine," Dani reassured her as she walked out the door.

She sat in her SUV finishing her notes, before pulling away. She drove over to Patty Fillmore's house, but she wasn't at home. Remembering she worked at the local bank downtown, she cut a U-turn and headed towards the center of town.

*

Two hours later, Dani finally arrived back at the sheriff's office building.

"Please tell me you have something," Sheriff Fisher said as she walked past his office. Dani turned around and walked inside.

"I talked to Larry's roommate. She hadn't seen him in a while because she works nights. Honestly, she didn't know much about him. I showed her Roger and Paul's photos and she'd seen them hanging out with Larry at the house though. I also found a couple of joints in his sock drawer."

"I just don't see pot being the reason behind all these murders. Hell, it's becoming legal in two or three more states this year," he huffed.

Dani shrugged. "The only thing they all had in common was the fact that they were friends and they were all into smoking pot, which Roger also grew, and Paul was a coke addict too."

"Did the roommate say anything about Larry traveling to the city?"

"No."

"Damn. Have you heard from Henry?"

"Not yet," she replied. "I did talk to Patty Fillmore though, Roger's ex-wife. She told me Larry came around from time to time when they were still married. He actually lived with them for a few months while he was trying to get on his feet about four years ago."

Sheriff Fisher blew out a frustrated breath and leaned back in his chair. "I may need to pick up a couple packs of cigarettes on the way home."

"I didn't know you smoked."

"I quit when I moved here. I was divorced and no longer a beat cop in the city, so my life was pretty stress free, and it has remained that way … until now."

Dani's cell phone rang before she could say anything. "Hey, Henry."

"Chief, I may have something for you."

"Wonderful. I'll be right there." She ended the call. "Henry thinks he has something."

"Thank God," he said, shaking his head.

"Hold off on the smokes. If we don't get this shit straightened out soon, I may have to light one up with you."

He laughed. "The day heath nut, Dani Ricketts, smokes a cigarette, is the day hell has frozen over."

She chuckled. "I'll call you in a bit."

Chapter 16

Dani walked into the hospital, wrinkling her nose at the horrible smell lingering in the hallway and getting stronger as she neared the morgue.

"Why the hell does he stink so bad?" she grimaced, plugging her nose.

"He's rotting. What did you expect? Flowers and perfume?" Henry shook his head and tossed her a small plastic jar of topical cream. "Spread that under your nose."

Dani raised an eyebrow.

"Just do it or quit bitching." He pushed his reading glasses up on his nose with the back of his hand.

Holding her breath, Dani opened the blue jar, stuck her finger into the gooey white substance and smeared it above her top lip. It tingled on her skin slightly. She closed the jar and set it on the counter before taking a shallow sniff like a dog checking something out. The extreme menthol scent burned her nostrils as she inhaled.

"I sent the toxicology screen out a little while ago. I'm not sure what you will get at this point. Most common street drugs don't stay in the bloodstream long."

"You said you found something?"

"Yes. He was hit on the head twice, here and then here." He pointed to the smashed and recently shaved skull of the body. "This first blow knocked him out and probably caused bleeding in his brain, but the second blow is what killed him. If you look at the angle, more than likely he was kneeling and turned his head and was hit. He fell to his side and then was struck again. The cylindrical shape of the indentions got me thinking about things that would be similar and used to whack someone in the head."

"Okay." Dani stepped back. Dead bodies weren't as exciting to her as they were to Henry.

"You see this second wound up here?" He pointed towards the skull. "You can't really see it with the naked eye, but the magnifying glass shows shapes recessed in the indention of the wound. I dusted the shapes with fingerprint ink, and this is what I got," he said, handing her a piece of thin stencil paper.

Dani looked at the paper and back at him, shrugging. He handed her a regular piece of paper that had an image that he'd printed from his computer. He moved her hands so that the stencil paper went overtop the regular paper. The words Genuine Louisville Slugger were clearly visible.

"Holy shit," she exclaimed.

"My thoughts exactly. You're looking for a wooden bat that probably has blood, hair, brain matter and other fibers stuck on it," he replied.

"What if the killer washed it?"

"It's wood and depending on how old it is … it could still have tissue embedded in it. If you find the bat, you find the killer."

Dani wrote a few notes in her notepad and cleaned the cream from her nose as she stepped outside. The sun was starting to set over the mountains in the distance. She placed a quick call to the sheriff to update him on the news of the weapon and headed home. She was just about to pull into the back parking area of her parent's store when Kristen's face popped into her head. She thought about turning around in the small lot and heading off in the opposite direction towards the lake but pulled into her usual parking space and cut the engine instead.

The skinny orange cat meowed when she walked inside, weaving in and out of her legs as she moved methodically through the apartment. She stripped her uniform and stepped into the shower, washing away the invisible stench of Larry's body that had been assaulting her senses all day.

"I need a vacation," she sighed, looking at the person staring back at her in the mirror as she brushed her towel-dried hair.

Her mind drifted to Kristen again. The image of her naked body covered with a light sheen of sweat made Dani's pulse race and her chest ache. Blowing out a frustrating breath, she tossed the brush onto the shelf next to the mirror before leaving the room and quickly dressed in jeans and a t-shirt.

*

Dani crossed the street, walking towards Muddy's to hopefully clear her head with a stiff drink, when a car riding by caught her eye. She cocked her head to the side, stopping her feet as the realization hit her. It was the same gray car that she'd chased out of town a week and a half ago. She started running towards the car, but the driver squealed the tires and disappeared down a side street.

"Fuck!" she yelled, reaching for her cell phone. She scrolled for the number to dispatch and waited for whoever was on shift to answer.

"Cypress Lake Sheriff's Office."

"This is Chief Ricketts. I need you to dispatch a BOLO for a two-door gray Nissan with tinted windows. I don't have a plate number, but the driver is male, and I just spotted the car at the corner of Eagle Road and Walnut Street."

"Yes, ma'am," the deputy said.

"Alert anyone on shift to proceed with caution. I believe this is the same car that evaded Deputy Nyman and I recently on a routine traffic stop."

Dani's mind flashed on Kristen as she ended the call. She turned around and jogged back towards her SUV.

*

Kristen was about to sit down and eat the grilled cheese sandwich she'd just made when a knock on the door startled her. She wasn't expecting anyone. She set the plate on the counter in the kitchen and padded across the living room to the front door.

"If you're here to tell me you made a mistake or feed me some excuse about why I haven't seen or heard from you in a week and a half, then you can get back in your truck and go home. I don't want to hear it," Kristen said, behind the screen door.

"Are you okay?" Dani asked, ignoring the jab.

"Okay? What the hell do you think? I don't know what's going on between us and a big part of me doesn't want to find out. I can't do this, Dani."

"I know we need to talk, but I'm here because I just saw that gray car again. He was over by my place and took off when I tried to approach the car. I was on foot, so he got away. I wanted to make sure you hadn't seen him tonight."

"No," Kristen replied, shaking her head. "I haven't been out in the last two days."

"There's something else," Dani added, pushing the handle on the screen door to go inside of the house, but it was locked.

"I said I didn't want to hear it, Dani. It's probably best if we both go our separate ways." Kristen found it difficult to peel her eyes away from the woman in front of her.

"Larry Hicks was found dead today with the side of his head smashed in."

"What? Oh my God." Kristen seemed visibly shaken as she unlocked the door and pushed it open.

Dani stepped inside and shoved the front door closed behind her before sitting down next to Kristen on the couch.

"What the hell is going on around here?" Kristen sighed.

"I don't know." Dani shrugged. "But I'm not going to let anyone hurt you."

Kristen saw the wild look in Dani's eyes, forgetting for a second the reason she was there. Her mind had replayed their night together more times than she could count and as much as she didn't want or need complications, her body yearned for the enticing woman next to her.

"Don't look at me like that," Kristen whispered, turning her gaze away from the eyes that stirred her to the core.

"I should go," Dani made a move to stand up. "I only stopped by to make sure you were okay."

Kristen grabbed her wrist. "No," she muttered, looking back at her. "I'm certainly not okay."

Dani's mouth watered and her pulse quickened.

Kristen stood up and stepped in front of Dani. "You make me crazy," she said seductively, moving to straddle her lap. She watched as a wicked grin crossed Dani's face.

Kristen had always been weak and powerless to that devilishly sexy smile, and this time was no different. She felt the wetness between her legs as Dani wrapped her arms around her, sliding her hands under the back of her shirt. Their lips met in a heated kiss that ignited the fire between them.

Dani pulled Kristen's shirt over her head, tossing it to the floor behind her as she ran her mouth over Kristen's jaw and down her neck. Unclasping her bra, she added it to the pile and moved her lips lower.

Kristen arched her body, trusting Dani's arms to hold her. She ran her hands through the silky strands of Dani's hair as Dani licked her breasts, sucking her nipples between her lips. She felt one of Dani's strong arms holding her as Dani's other hand grazed the side of her breast, slipping down her stomach to the waistband of her shorts.

Dani pushed her hand into Kristen's shorts, moaning as she dipped her fingers into the warm wetness she knew was awaiting her. Kristen's body jerked at the sensitive touch and then relaxed as Dani's fingers moved back and forth over her clit. She rocked against the hand touching her, searching for more contact.

Dani made a sudden move to the side, swinging Kristen back onto the couch as she moved over her. She freed her hand, pulling Kristen's shorts and panties from her legs. Kristen sat up, unbuttoning Dani's jeans and pushing them down her legs as she removed her own t-shirt. Dani finally moved over her, skin touching skin as their lips met once more.

Kristen ran her hands over Dani's back, from her shoulders down to her ass, squeezing the muscled cheeks before slipping one hand between their bodies. Dani lifted her hips slightly, allowing Kristen the access she was

137

seeking. She mimicked her, sliding her fingers through Kristen's wetness again before pushing them inside. Kristen parted her thighs wider, urging her deeper, while working her fingers towards Dani's entrance. Dani kissed her hard, moaning into her mouth as Kristen plunged into her.

Both women panted between lustful kisses, rocking back and forth, while working in and out of each other as a light sheen of sweat covered their skin. The feeling of Kristen's body tightening around her fingers made Dani lose control of the orgasm building below the surface. Unable to hold on, she gripped the couch under Kristen and bit down on her bottom lip as the powerful climax roared through her body.

Kristen wrapped her arm tightly around Dani, holding on for the ride as her body let go simultaneously. She moaned loudly, begging for more as Dani stroked the last wave of pleasure from her willing body before collapsing on top of her.

Dani was spent. She struggled to regain control as they carefully removed their fingers from each other. Kristen put her clean hand on Dani's cheek, turning her chin up so she could see the turbulent green eyes that had repeatedly unhinged her with a simple look. Dani smiled affectionately before kissing her softly.

Kristen yelped when Dani tried to move to her side. Their sweaty skin had melded together, causing them to literally peel apart as they separated. Dani grinned, running her hand down the center of Kristen's chest and fanning it out over her stomach.

Kristen moved up onto her side, allowing Dani to have more room on the wide couch as she moved over her. "Stay with me," she whispered, biting her lower lip as she met Dani's eyes once more.

Dani pulled Kristen down, answering her with a searing kiss.

Chapter 17

Dani awoke well before sunrise, staring around the darkened room at her unusual surroundings. Kristen stirred next to her, bringing her mind back to their night spent together. She fumbled around in the darkness, trying not to wake the slumbering woman, but she bumped into the dresser, causing something to crash loudly against the hardwood floor.

Kristen sat up dazed and confused as if someone had slapped her.

"I'm sorry. I was trying not to wake you," Dani said softly.

"Where are you going? It's still dark out."

"To work. I have to be on shift in an hour." Dani moved to walk back over to the bed but stopped when her foot kicked the object that had caused all of the noise.

"Well, at least turn the light on before you kill yourself," Kristen chided.

"I didn't want to wake you." Dani raised an eyebrow, feeling the long cylindrical piece of wood.

"I'm up now," Kristen grimaced as she turned on the bedside lamp. "What are you doing with that?" she questioned. Dani was standing on the other side of the room, nude and holding a wooden bat.

Dani examined the old baseball bat in her hand. The end had the words Genuine Louisville Slugger stamped into it. She raised an eyebrow, looking back at Kristen. "This is what woke you up. Apparently, I knocked it over. What are you doing with it?"

"Since my gun was stolen, I needed something to protect me in case whoever is following me decides to make an appearance," Kristen shrugged.

"Where did it come from?"

"I got it out of the attic a couple weeks ago. It's the one we used to play ball with."

"Oh, yeah, I remember that," Dani replied, setting the bat back against the dresser.

"Didn't you have one too?" Kristen asked, getting out of bed.

"Yep, but I lost it when I moved out of my parent's house I think," she answered, opening her arms as Kristen stepped into them.

"Do you really have to go?" Kristen kissed her softly.

Dani closed her eyes. Nothing had ever felt as good as holding Kristen's naked body against hers. Still, she had work to do and as much as she hated to admit it, Kristen was coincidentally looking more and more like a suspect. She knew the truth and she knew Kristen, but if anyone else ever caught onto what she knew, Kristen would no doubt be arrested and charged for the three murders. Dani kissed her back before pulling away.

"I really need to go. I can't be late, and I still have to shower."

"Alright," Kristen sighed. "Come by later. I'll make dinner," she said, donning her robe as she followed Dani down the stairs.

"It's a date." Dani smiled, redressing quickly.

*

Dani walked into the sheriff's office with five minutes to spare. Her neck was slightly stiff, and she was tired from only having had a few hours of sleep. She remembered the way her and Kristen had given themselves to each other over and over. The thoughts both scared and excited her. She wasn't sure how much longer they could go on, passing like ships in the night, without someone getting hurt. She needed to talk to her and soon, before she fell any further.

"You're late," Sheriff Fisher called from her doorway.

Dani looked up at him. "No, I'm not," she replied, checking her watch.

"In the last three years, you've never come in later than half an hour before your shift."

She shrugged. "I slept in."

"Or didn't sleep at all," he grinned.

"What's that supposed to mean?" she growled.

"Deputy Wagner is coming off the night shift. Ask him," he said, walking away.

"Shit," she muttered to the empty room as she stood up from her desk.

After the shift change, Dani walked outside and leaned her back against Deputy Wagner's cruiser. She was standing with her arms crossed and her eyes hidden behind dark sunglasses as he moved towards her.

"Is there anything you want to tell me, Vince?"

"No," he shook his head.

"Are you sure?"

"Uh huh." The young, redheaded deputy swallowed the lump in his throat.

"So, Sheriff Fisher is lying then?"

"No. I don't know. What did he say?"

"There is nothing I hate more than town gossip," she said, raising her voice.

"I'm sorry. I—"

"Do you know where starting rumors gets you, Vince?" She glared at him behind the dark lenses. "Fired!" she yelled.

His beady eyes were large, and a bead of sweat had broken out on his brow; two distinctive signs that he was nervous.

"Next time, I suggest you keep things to yourself unless they pertain to you. Not that it's any of your business, but Kristin Malone and I have been friends since childhood and the gray car that Wilbur and I chased a few weeks ago has been following her around town. I went over to check on her last night after seeing the car in town again. She was a little shaken up when I told her and I stayed the night."

"I'm really sorry, Chief. I … all I said was I saw your cruiser parked at a lake house in the middle of the night. Sheriff Fisher asked which one and I told him. I assumed he knew you were there."

Dani shook her head. "Do you see what happens when you assume? You make an ass out of yourself. My whereabouts when I'm not on shift isn't anyone's business but my own."

"It won't happen again," he squeaked.

"You're damn right it won't," she seethed. *Next time, I'll take this fucking badge off and beat your ass, you little weasel!* "Get out of here," she said angrily as she pushed off his car and walked back inside. She moved her sunglasses up on her head.

"You scared the life out of that kid," Sheriff Fisher laughed when she walked past him.

Dani spun around and raised an eyebrow.

"I don't care to become a part of the town gossip."

"No one else knows. He mentioned he saw your SUV at her house, and I told him you were friends. That's all that was said. I was only jerking your chain to see if I could get a rise out of you."

"He shouldn't be worried about where my vehicle is and if he has a question, then he needs to ask me and that goes for you too. You know how much I hate rumors."

"I'm sure the town already knows. You forget Mrs. Cranston is her neighbor."

Dani rolled her eyes. "That old kook has known me since I was a kid, and she watched Kristen and I grow up together around that house."

"There's no reason to get so defensive, Dani. I know you're gay. Hell, most of the town probably does and if you two are together, then I'm happy for you, but you're right, it's no one's business."

This was the last thing Dani needed this morning and had definitely been the last thing she'd expected when she walked into the office. Ignoring his comment, she changed the subject. "I was there because that damn gray car was back in town last night. I saw him over by my house and I went to check on her."

"Has she seen him again?"

"No, not recently, but she wasn't exactly thrilled to know he was back." She turned to walk away. "What time is the meeting with the mayor?" she called back over her shoulder.

"One," he answered.

*

Dani had all but forgotten about the events of the morning, although her mind slipped back to Kristen from time to time as the day went on. She arrived at the mayor's office slightly before Sheriff Fisher. The warm sunshine of the spring day made her want to curl up and take a catnap. She pushed her sunglasses up on her head and yawned as she got out of her SUV.

"Don't start," she said, seeing the sheriff smile out the corner of her eye.

He shrugged, walking inside behind her. They waited in the lobby of Town Hall while the mayor's assistant informed him of their arrival. She returned a few minutes later and showed them to his office.

Mayor Olsen scratched the side of his more salt than pepper beard. "Do either of you care to explain to me why people keep turning up dead in my town?"

"Roger, Paul, and Larry were all friends and they all dabbled in drugs. My contact with the city police department told me one of their lowball operations had been trying to run drugs using outside sources. My guess is these three decided to jump on board and more than likely Paul screwed them over and hence, three dead guys," Dani spoke up.

"I'm not buying it," Mayor Olsen replied, shaking his head.

"Well, it's not a serial killer; none of the M.O.'s match. It could be a coincidence that these guys happened to know each other. Most of the town knows each other. It could be three random murders. Hell, for all we know, Roger killed Paul and Larry killed Roger," Sheriff Fisher countered.

"Then who the fuck killed Larry? Paul's ghost?" Mayor Olsen smacked the top of his desk with the palm of his hand.

"Well, who else were they friends with? Maybe someone else was caught up in their little circle and if they screwed each other over, then maybe whoever is left killed Larry." Dani shrugged.

"None of this makes any Goddamn sense."

"Mayor Olsen, we do have a possible weapon in Larry's case. He was killed with a Louisville Slugger, literally. Part of the wording was embedding into his head," Sheriff Fisher informed him.

"What are we supposed to do, arrest everyone in town with a wooden bat?" he sneered.

"There is also one other thing," Dani added. "We've had a suspicious car riding around town. In fact, it followed Kristin Malone on more than one occasion. We know the driver is male, but he led us on a chase to the town limits the only time we were able to perform a traffic stop. I'm pretty sure whoever is driving this car is not a resident of Cypress Lake. I've run a search on the vehicle, and we don't have any cars fitting the description registered here. Whoever he is, he knows his way around town and he's been seen near the times that each body has been found. I have a very strong feeling this person is who we should be looking at for these murders. Whether he's with a drug ring or not, it doesn't matter at this point. I believe he's our only suspect."

"It's time you followed my orders and stepped-up patrols, Fisher. Use roadblocks or any other means necessary but stop this son of a bitch the next time he appears within our town limits. If he runs again, shoot his tires out," Mayor Olsen growled.

"It's your call," Sheriff Fisher replied.

"I don't give a damn about the budget. I want this guy stopped!"

"You heard him, Chief. Any means necessary."

Dani nodded.

A few minutes later, Dani followed Sheriff Fisher out of the building and into the bright sunshine. She pulled her dark glasses back down, shading her eyes.

"We have to stop this guy, Ricketts. After finding out he was back again last night, I agree with you. He's our only suspect."

"I'll radio dispatch now for another BOLO for the car and as soon as I get back to the office I'll go back over the schedule and start pulling people in for twelve-hour rotations," she said as she climbed into her vehicle.

Chapter 18

Dani spent the rest of the afternoon adjusting the schedule and briefing everyone about the changes and the vehicle they were after. She remembered her dinner plans with Kristen at the last minute as she was turning into the parking lot behind her parents' store.

"Shit!" she exclaimed, grabbing her phone and scrolling for Kristen's number as she spun around and sped off in the opposite direction.

"I'm sorry. I had a crazy day. I'm headed your way now," she said when the line was answered.

"It's okay. I haven't started cooking yet anyway," Kristen replied.

Ten minutes later, Kristen heard the knock at the door, and she was surprised to see Dani still in her uniform when she pulled it open.

"Hey." Kristen unlocked the screen. "You look tired," she frowned as Dani stepped inside.

Dani looked back at her with a raised eyebrow. "I didn't sleep much last night, which the sheriff knows by the way, and I just got out of a meeting with the mayor."

"What do you mean the sheriff knows? What does he know?"

"Where I was last night. One of my deputies saw my cruiser here in the middle of the night while he was on patrol and informed Sheriff Fisher this morning."

"That's wonderful," Kristen said sarcastically, shaking her head.

"I scared the life out of the deputy, so hopefully the rumor mill won't get wind of it. Sheriff Fisher, on the other hand, was jerking my chain pretty good. He knows about me and made a correct assumption. I played it off on account of us being friends though, but he's not stupid."

"I hate this damn town," Kristen growled.

"Larry's murder has the mayor's panties in a bunch. I really think whoever is driving the fucking gray car is involved, but at this point we may never see him again. We've moved to rotating twelve-hour shifts and extra patrols until we catch this bastard," Dani sighed.

"Do you think he's the killer?"

"I have no idea." Dani shrugged. "Three people are dead and the car mysteriously appears each time we find a body. What I don't understand, is why he's been following you around."

Kristen ran a shaky hand through her hair. "I think I know."

"What do you mean?"

Kristen grabbed Dani's hand and pulled her over to the couch to sit down. "I haven't been completely honest with you," she said, swallowing the lump in her throat.

Dani raised an eyebrow, watching the turmoil cross Kristen's face.

"I'm here against my parents' wishes. They gave me the house a few years ago, knowing I'd eventually sell it. When I told them I was coming back to make sure we hadn't left anything behind and to put the house on the auction block, they begged me not to return, but I needed closure."

"Do they hate me that much? What the hell did they think I'd do, kidnap you?" Dani huffed.

"No." Kristen shook her head. "They loved you like a daughter, Dani. Tearing us apart was hard for them, but they didn't know what else to do."

Dani cocked her head to the side. "I don't understand—"

"I lied to you. I'm sorry. I was supposed to come here, do what I needed to do and get out. I never anticipated seeing you again." Kristen sighed.

"How does this have anything to do with the murders?"

"Dani, my parents didn't move me away from here because you and I were together. They did it because I was gang raped by four guys," she said softly as tears began to fall from her eyes.

Dani jerked her head. "What?"

"Right after spring break, I was walking to your house to surprise you and a car stopped me, offering me a ride. I knew the guys, so I thought it was safe. They took turns raping me while the others held me down. When they were finished, they dumped me in the parking lot of Barber's."

"Oh my God," Dani whispered, wiping the tears from her face.

"My parents took me to the hospital in the city, and then to my aunt's from there. They stayed here long enough to pack up the house and rent it out, before moving for good. I wanted to call you so badly, but I was scared to death they would kill me. I found out I was pregnant a few weeks later and had an abortion not long after that."

"I ... I don't know what to say, Kristen. I'm sorry that happened to you." Dani pulled Kristen into her arms. "I couldn't imagine going through something like that."

"I'm so sorry I never contacted you. I loved you so damn much. That's why it has taken me so long to come back. I couldn't handle being in town and I didn't know how to face you."

Kristen closed her eyes; Dani's arms had always been the only place she'd ever felt safe. "It's no excuse for breaking your heart though."

"I wish I could've been there for you. I loved you more than anything in the world. You could've told me."

"I wanted to. I picked up the phone so many times, but I was scared. I didn't want to be anywhere near here and I knew if I talked to you, I'd want to see you. Anyway, it's in the past now ... or at least it was," Kristen said, pulling away.

Dani watched Kristen's face, waiting for her to look up. Kristen finally met her eyes, sighing softly.

"Paul Davis, Roger Fillmore, and Larry Hicks were the guys that raped me."

"What?" Dani stiffened. "Are you sure?"

"Yes."

Dani shook her head. "This is bad."

"I know. That's why I'm telling you this. I never wanted you to know what happened to me, but now, with these guys turning up dead, I figured I had better tell you the truth."

"You knew the three dead guys, you have two of the murder weapons, and now you have a motive," Dani said. She stood, turning around to face her. "Son of a bitch, Kristen!"

"What do you mean I have the murder weapons? I didn't kill those guys, Dani. Sure, I wished them dead many times over, but I didn't do this."

"Roger was shot with a .380 or 9mm and Larry's head was smashed in with a bat that left an imprint. You had a handgun matching the caliber and you have a bat that matches the logo imprinted on Larry's skull."

"My house was broken into, and my gun was stolen."

"The break-in could've easily been staged."

"Oh my God, are you seriously standing here telling me you think I did this?" Kristen growled as she jumped to her feet.

"I don't know what to think. All I do know, is you're a suspect and there is enough evidence for me to arrest you and charge you with at least two of the murders."

"I can't believe this. I came back here to get closure. I need to get rid of this place and put this fucking town behind me. I can't go on with my life until I do." Kristen paced the floor. "This is absurd. Dani, look at me. Do you honestly think I'm capable of killing three grown men?"

"You're easily capable of pulling a trigger and swinging a bat, so yes."

"What about the guy in the gray car? You saw him too, so you know I'm not making that up."

"I know and that's why I'm giving you the benefit of the doubt."

"I told you four guys raped me and I think it's him in that car. He obviously knows I'm back and he's either trying to scare me or kill me. I think he killed the other three and made it look like it was me on purpose."

"I'm not going to let anyone hurt you ever again. I'll protect you just like I always have."

"What do you mean?"

"After you left in such a haste, and then your family followed, rumors swirled around. I didn't know what had happened, but I tamped the rumors down and stood up for you anyway. Eventually it became old news."

"God, I hate this town." Kristen blew out a frustrating breath and ran her hand through her hair.

"What did you say the fourth guy's name was?" Dani asked.

"I didn't … but it was Steve Olsen."

Dani was stunned. "Are you sure?"

Kristen raised an eyebrow. "I'll never forget their faces."

Dani shook her head. "You know he's the mayor's son."

"Yes, and back when he raped me, he was the sheriff's son. That's why my parents took me away from here. They thought the guys would get away with it."

"Steve hasn't been around in a couple of years. He took a job out of town somewhere when his parents got divorced. No one has seen him since he moved away," Dani said, walking over to the window and staring out at the light on the end of the dock. She was glad the gray car had evaded the routine stop by one of her deputies, otherwise she would be hauling Kristen down to the sheriff's office right now on murder charges with a circumstantial case strong enough to lock her away for a long time, if not get her the death penalty. She wasn't sure what to do. If anyone else found out about this, gray car or not, she'd have to arrest Kristen.

Kristen sat back down on the couch with her head in her hands. She had just put her life in Dani's hands, hoping she believed her. She thought about taking off in the middle of the night and forgetting about the old possessions in the attic that she'd been slowly packing up.

"This has to stay between us," Dani said, walking away from the window and back towards her. "If anyone in the sheriff's office finds out about what you just told me, I won't be able to protect you."

Kristen nodded. She knew Dani was putting her career on the line for her.

"I should get going. I need to get some sleep." Dani yawned. Although she was definitely tired, she needed to digest all the information swirling around in her head.

"Okay," Kristen replied, walking her to the door.

Dani pulled Kristen into her arms, kissing the side of her head at her temple. "I meant what I said. I'm not going to let anyone hurt you ever again."

Kristen closed her eyes, sinking into the woman holding her.

Chapter 19

Dani spent the next two weeks working the crazy schedule of rotating shifts. She tried to see Kristen as much as she could, but most days, she went home and fell asleep on the couch before she could eat dinner. The mysterious car hadn't been spotted, and she was beginning to wonder if it ever would again. She walked into her office, tossing the trash she'd cleaned out of her SUV into the waste basket.

"You look about as tired as I feel," Sheriff Fisher said, leaning against the wall in the hallway with his arms crossed.

"I think we're wasting man hours. We may never see that car again and honestly, I'd be happy with that."

"What about the unsolved murders?" Sheriff Fisher asked, pursing his lips.

"I understand that no murder goes unnoticed and I took the same oath you did, but these guys weren't exactly upstanding citizens of Cypress Lake, and they obviously got themselves into a lot of trouble. Now, we're potentially wasting our time and our budget for something that could easily be nothing."

"I agree with you there. I have a feeling we'll never see that car again." He pushed off the wall. "We're going back to our regular schedule after next week."

Dani nodded. "What about Mayor Olsen?"

Sheriff Fisher shrugged. "If he doesn't like it, then he can fire me."

*

Dani walked into her apartment, wiping the sweat from her forehead. The summer heat had finally begun. She peeled out of her uniform and pulled on shorts and a t-shirt as she perused the refrigerator.

"I need to teach you how to grocery shop," she said to the cat who was standing on the small kitchen table, meowing at her. "You'll have to settle for a can of tuna fish. You're out of food." She opened the can and lumped the slightly pink contents into his bowl. The cat hopped down and turned his nose up at his bowl before walking away.

"That's why I named you Asshole!" She growled at him as she pushed her wallet and cell phone into her pockets and snatched her keys off the counter.

After a few knocks on the back door of the store, Dani's father finally let her in.

"Hey," he said, hugging her.

"Hi, Dad."

"Any news on those murders?" he asked, sitting back down at his desk.

"No. The suspect is probably long gone. I still think its drug related. Those guys weren't worth a shit to anyone and probably screwed over a dealer in the city. We're going back to our regular schedule next week."

Her father shook his head. "Your mom's been happy to see the extra patrols, so I wouldn't mention anything about that to her. You know how she worries about you."

Dani grabbed one of the extra baskets from the back. "That damn cat won't eat tuna fish," she exclaimed when he raised an eyebrow.

Her father laughed. "Get him something from the deli."

"He's lucky he's not homeless and rummaging through the trash for scraps," she huffed, pushing through the double doors and walking out into the store.

Dani walked down the animal aisle and picked out a dozen cans of cat food before going down a few more aisles to get some extra things for herself. Her mother was checking in a frozen food order, so Dani said hey to her quickly and headed up to the cashier.

"Hey, stranger."

Dani felt the presence behind her before she heard the voice. She spun around to see Kristen standing there with an adorable smile on her face.

"Hi. What brings you out this evening?" Dani asked, wanting to kiss her so badly, but thought better of it since they were standing in the checkout line with people around.

"The same thing as you, groceries," Kristen replied, peering into her basket as Dani began putting her items on the conveyer. She raised her eyebrow. "What's with all of the cat food?"

Dani rolled her eyes. "That damn cat of mine is a picky eater and thinks he's some kind of feline God or something and I should bow down and kiss his hairy paws."

"Cat? I didn't know you had a cat."

"Long story."

"What else don't I know about you?"

Dani shrugged.

"You live upstairs, right?"

"Yes." Dani handed the cashier her bank card from her wallet and leaned closer to Kristen, trying not to be overheard. "Do you want to come up?"

"Sure. I'll see you in a bit," Kristen answered as the cashier began scanning her items. She was glad she hadn't picked up anything that needed to be refrigerated as she watched Dani walk away with her bags.

Kristen hadn't planned on rekindling her relationship with Dani or even seeing her again at all for that matter, but she couldn't deny the strong attraction and resurrected feelings. She'd learned weeks ago that avoiding the yearning deep inside of her only made it worse. She was falling all over again, fast and hard and she didn't know how to stop or if she even wanted to.

*

Dani showed Kristen around her studio apartment, and they made a spaghetti dinner together, after feeding the cat, of course. Kristen didn't act at all surprised to see Dani's neat and tidy lifestyle. She'd never been a flamboyant person to begin with, so the cozy apartment fit her.

"I can't get over you having a cat. You were never a cat person," Kristen said while petting the feline.

"I'm still not, but I couldn't leave him to die of hunger or get run over by a car."

"Well, who names their cat, Asshole Cat?"

"People who get bitten by their asshole cats," Dani answered, walking up behind her. She brushed Kristen's hair to the side and kissed the back of her neck softly.

Kristen moaned and leaned back into her.

"Since you like petting cats so much, I have another cat you can pet," Dani teased. "It's nowhere near as hairy and doesn't bite," she finished, wrapping her arms around Kristen's waist as she placed more kisses along her neck and near her ear.

Kristen could no longer take the assault on her sensitive skin. She spun in Dani's arms, pushing her back towards her bed on the opposite side of the room. Dani landed on her back and Kristen crawled up on top of her, straddling her hips. She grabbed Dani's hands and held them down on her own thighs.

"Where is this going?" Kristen murmured.

"Hopefully, to the land of naked orgasms and rather quickly," Dani answered, trying to move her hands.

"I'm serious, Dani. We need to talk about what's going on between us."

"I don't know, Kristen." Dani sat up. "Having you back in my life has been a blessing and a curse."

"Why?"

"I love having you around. You make me feel complete, but I know you're not back permanently and eventually you will leave again, shattering my heart to pieces once more when you do."

"Wow." Kristen slid off her and sat to the side.

"I accepted this a while ago, when I knew I couldn't control my attraction to you. It is what it is."

Kristen looked stunned, like she'd just been slapped across the face.

"I'm not trying to be mean, Kristen, just honest … brutally honest, with myself and with you."

"So where does this leave us?"

"I don't know. I guess we'll cross that bridge or burn it down when we get there," Dani replied.

"Have you ever thought of moving to the city?"

"No. Duplexes, Walmart, and thousands of people, really aren't for me."

"How do you know if you've never tried it?"

"I went to college, Kristen. I lived in the city for four years and I hated it. I came home every weekend and moved back the day after graduation."

Kristen backed away slightly. "You went to the university in the city?"

"No. I went to the private college," Dani explained, referring to the large private institution in another outlying city that was slightly smaller than the one Kristen had moved to. "I've been to the city you live in though. Two hours isn't that far of a drive."

"When were you there?"

"When I first left for college. I had to make sure you were okay."

"What do you mean? How did you know where I was?" Kristen raised an eyebrow, swallowing the lump in her throat.

"I was so torn when you left, and I didn't know what to do. I went to your parents' house every day looking for you and they finally told me everything."

"Everything?"

"About the attack and said you moved to the city with your mom's sister."

Kristen stood up. Her parents had always said no one knew and that they left without giving a reason to anyone. She stared at Dani, confused and visibly shaken.

"Are you okay?" Dani asked, standing up and going to her.

"Yeah. I'm a little shocked, I guess. I don't feel well. Maybe I'm coming down with something."

"Do you want me to get you something to drink?"

"No. I should probably go home and lie down. You have to be up early for work anyway."

"Are you sure?"

"Yes. I'll be fine." Kristen hugged her. "I'll call you tomorrow."

Kristen knew something wasn't right about what Dani had said to her. She dialed her parents' number as soon as she got into her car. Her mother answered on the second ring.

"Hey, darling."

"Hi, Mom. Do you remember I told you I ran into Dani recently?"

"Yes."

"When everything happened and I moved away, did you or Dad ever tell her about it before you left?"

"No. We didn't say anything to anyone. In fact, we barely saw Dani. She came looking for you and we told her you went to visit a sick relative and left it at that. We were gone the following week."

"Okay, thanks."

"Did she say anything about it?"

"No. I was just thinking of telling her."

"Why stir up the past, honey? You two are both better off. You have a great life now up here. I wish you'd leave that old place alone and come home."

"I'm almost done. In fact, I'll probably be leaving soon."

"Good. Let's plan for dinner when you get back."

Kristen pulled into the driveway of her lake house, ending the call as she walked inside. She felt deflated, like the last eight weeks had been one huge blur. She didn't know who was lying, Dani or her mother, but one of them wasn't telling her the truth and she had no idea why either one would lie to her in the first place. Her mother had nothing to gain or lose now if she'd told her daughter's secret twelve years ago. Then again, why would Dani have a reason to lie about knowing what had happened? The entire situation made her head hurt.

Chapter 20

The next afternoon, Dani was sitting at her desk, writing up the new schedule for the following week since they were going back to their regular hours. She looked up from her computer when she heard a knock on the wall. Sheriff Fisher was leaning against the door frame.

"Nyman and Wagner both called out for second shift. Apparently, they picked up a nasty stomach bug and are puking and shitting everywhere."

Dani grimaced. "You could've spared me the details."

He laughed. "Figure out who you can put on the second half of the overnight shift and then take off after you finish what you're working on so you can get some sleep and cover the first half tonight."

"Dewitt is available. I'll call him in."

"Alright." He nodded, walking away.

*

A half hour later, Dani had made the call to the deputy and finished filling in the boxes on the schedule spreadsheet. She was headed home when she decided to take a detour across town. Kristen's blue car was parked in the driveway and Dani pulled her SUV in behind it.

Dani barely knocked on the door before it swung open.

Kristen looked slightly shaken. Despite all the thoughts of lies swirling in her head, she couldn't stop the instant arousal she felt from seeing Dani. "Hi … what are you doing here?"

"You don't look very happy to see me. Is something wrong?" Dani asked, pushing her sunglasses up on her head.

"I'm fine. Aren't you supposed to be working?"

"No. We have some guys out sick, so I switched my schedule around to help cover the shift."

"Oh."

"I can go if you're busy. I was thinking about you, so I thought I'd stop by. I should've called first," Dani sighed, sensing something was bothering Kristen.

"It's fine. I'm glad you're here." Kristen kissed her lips softly, and then backed away, walking into the kitchen. "I talked to my mom this morning. Are you sure she's the one who told you about what happened to me? She said she and my dad never said anything to anyone."

Dani raised an eyebrow as she sat down on one of the bar stools on the opposite side of the counter that Kristen was leaning on. "Maybe she forgot. It was a long time ago. Anyway, it doesn't matter."

"It matters to me, Dani."

"I think the fact that three of the guys are dead and you're the prime suspect is a little more important at this point. Don't you?" Dani countered, watching the shadow cross Kristen's face. "No one in town knows what happened then and now, except for the two of us. If the sheriff finds out, you'll most certainly get the death penalty."

"I ... I didn't kill those guys," Kristen's voice cracked with fear. "This is crazy."

Dani slid off the stool and walked around the counter, pulling Kristen into her arms. She closed her eyes, inhaling the scent of light perfume mixed with shampoo. "You don't have to convince me, Kristen. I know you didn't kill them, and nothing is going to happen to you. I won't let it."

Kristen wasn't sure what she meant, but she was too distraught to question her.

Dani kissed the side of her head and backed away. "Don't worry, everything will be fine. I promise."

Kristen mustered a smile.

"I need to go so I can grab something to eat. I have to be back on shift in a few hours."

Kristen walked her to the door, kissing her tenderly before she left. She watched through the window as Dani climbed into her SUV and drove away. She wished she could listen to her and believe what she was saying, but something didn't feel right, and she trusted her gut instinct. Dani wasn't being completely honest and the more she thought about it, the more it scared the hell out of her.

*

Kristen spent the rest of the day and most of the night trying to rationalize the thoughts in her head, but nothing added up. She knew there was more to the story. Dani somehow knew what had happened to her and now, she was the one investigating the murders of three of the guys involved. Dani held all the cards. Kristen's mind began to wonder.

"Oh my God," she whispered as she ran a trembling hand through her hair.

She ran upstairs, quickly grabbed her suitcase and spread it open onto her bed. The clock on the nightstand flashed twelve-fifteen a.m. in big red numbers. She began throwing her clothes into the bag in disarray. The more she thought about the dead guys and Dani, the more she wanted to get as far away as possible. A few minutes later, Kristen tossed her bag into the backseat of the car and set her phone in the cup holder.

"Shit," she said, smacking the steering wheel when she saw that she only had a quarter of a tank.

She turned off Lake Drive and headed towards the nearest gas station to fill up. The eerie roads were dark and empty in the middle of the night. She hastily grabbed a large cup of coffee from inside the store as the gas pump automatically filled her car up. She then sped off towards the main road that would take her out of town and towards the interstate. She kept the radio off as she drove.

She watched the woods thicken on either side of the road as Cypress Lake slid further and further behind her. She was just about to the town limit when she saw headlights in her rearview mirror, then blue lights flashing.

"Fuck!" she yelled, pulling over. She pushed the button to roll her window down as she nervously watched the side mirror as the deputy walked towards her car. She knew who it was by the fit of the uniform. *Damn it.*

"Kristen?" Dani appeared stunned. "What are you doing out here in the middle of the night?" She looked around inside of the car, noticing the bag in the back and the coffee in the console.

"There's an emergency at home," Kristen said, avoiding the eyes she knew could see right through to her soul.

Dani raised her eyebrow and cocked her head to the side. "What happened?"

"I don't know."

Dani nodded. "So, you're heading to the city in the middle of the night for an emergency, but you don't know what it is?"

"Just let me go, Dani. Please," Kristen pleaded.

"Why are you running away? Don't do this. I love you, Kristen. I don't want to lose you again. Don't go," Dani urged.

Kristen felt a tear roll down her face when she finally met Dani's eyes. "I can't take all the lies, Dani. I don't know what's real anymore."

"Whose lying?"

"You are!"

"I've never lied to you, Kristen."

Kristen wiped her tears away angrily. "You're keeping things from me. I don't even know who you are anymore."

"What do you want from me?" Dani asked.

"I want the truth, Dani. I have all these questions and you keep talking in riddles."

Dani checked her watch, her half of the shift had ended a few minutes ago. "Can we at least go to your house and talk? I'll tell you whatever you want to know."

"Fine," Kristen said, rolling up her window.

Dani ran back to her SUV and pulled out onto the road behind Kristen. She grabbed the microphone on the side of the computer and radioed dispatch to make sure her replacement had signed on, and then she signed off for the night. Dani hated seeing the sadness on Kristen's face and the fear in her eyes. Knowing she was the one who had put it there tore her up. Hurting Kristen was the last thing she'd ever wanted to do. She followed the small blue car silently through the dark streets and turned into the driveway behind it.

Kristen left her suitcase in the car as she moved to unlock the front door of the house. The left bag didn't go unnoticed as Dani walked inside behind her. Kristen turned on the living room lights and sat down on the chair adjacent to the sofa where Dani sat.

Dani's green eyes swirled wildly when Kristen looked at her and spoke. "Tell me the truth, Dani. How did you find out about what happened to me?"

"Roger, Paul and Larry came to school joking about what they'd done the following week. I overheard them talking about how you screamed and begged them to stop while you cried for me over and over."

"Oh my God," Kristen put her hand over her heart as the memories flooded back to her. She wiped a tear from her face that had fallen from her moist eyes.

Dani sighed. "I never got over what they did to you. They needed to be punished."

Kristen sat back in the chair. "What do you mean? Dani, did you do something to them?" she asked nervously.

"Are you glad they're dead?" Dani asked.

"It was twelve years ago. This isn't the closure that I came back for. I've moved on with my life."

"How could you move on away from me? You never even said goodbye."

"It wasn't easy, but I was forced to live a different life when I moved away. I figured you got on with your life too."

"I kept tabs on them over years after I joined the sheriff's office. I swore I'd never let them hurt anyone else."

"Is this why you became a deputy?" Kristen asked.

"Yes," Dani replied, looking her in the eyes. "It's also why I had to find you and make sure you were okay."

"Oh, Dani," she sighed, reaching out and squeezing Dani's hand. "Why didn't you say anything when you saw me?"

"You looked happy ... without me." Dani shrugged. "I came home and went back to my life."

"Every time I thought of you, I thought of this place and that night always came back to me. I had to let go of you, of everything, so that I could move on."

"I know. I hated them too, probably as much as you did, but I vowed to keep the town safe, so I watched Roger, Paul, and Larry live their lives, dabbling in and out drugs over the years, praying that they overdosed or pissed off the wrong dealer. They finally parted ways and barely spent any time together in the past four years, but right before Paul's body was found the three of them started getting together again. I assumed they'd found out you were back in town. I never knew there were four of them involved in your attack though. Steve Olsen wasn't around those three much during the last few months of school and I never saw him with them after graduation. Then, he moved away."

"Did you know I was back?"

"No, not at first. I noticed them meet up twice in one week and the timeframe coincided with the prowler call at your house. I pulled the record from the call and saw your name. That's when I knew you'd returned."

"Were they coming after me?" she whispered.

"I have no idea," Dani said.

"Did you have anything to do with what happened to them?"

"No, but they're gone, and they can't hurt you ever again. Isn't that all that matters?"

"I don't know. This is a lot to take in." Kristen shivered with fear. She wasn't sure she believed her. It scared her to think Dani may have been the one who brutally murdered the three guys. She was certainly capable of doing it.

"I love you, Kristen. I'd never do anything to hurt you. I should've told you everything when I found out you were in town. I didn't know what to do. I thought I'd never see you again."

"I never expected to see you when I came back. I planned to be here for a few weeks to tie up some loose ends with the auction for the house and pack up the stuff my family had left behind. Then, you came back into my life. I've always loved you, Dani, and seeing you again resurrected all the old feelings I thought I'd buried away forever, but this mess, whatever it is that's going on here—" She spread her arms around. "It scares the hell out of me. I can't help feeling like someone is out there trying to hurt me and you're right in the middle of it all."

Dani lowered her head. "I'd take it all away if I could."

"I know," Kristen said, moving to the couch next to her. As scared as Kristen was of her at the moment, the love she felt deep inside for Dani prevailed.

Dani wrapped her arms around Kristen and held her tightly.

Chapter 21

Dani spent every waking minute of the next two days combing the town for any trace of Steve Olsen. She checked with the bank to see if his account had any recent activity, but the last transaction on record was three years ago. She didn't know much about Steve since she hadn't known he was involved with Kristen's attack, so she spent countless hours visiting old classmates and other acquaintances that also knew Steve. She even rode past the mayor's house every couple of hours, hoping to see Steve's car in the driveway. She also talked to Larry's roommate and Roger's ex-wife to see if either of them had ever seen him around. No one in Cypress Lake had seen Steve Olsen in three years.

*

Kristen was starting to wonder if Steve really was back and trying to hurt her or if Dani was more involved than she was letting on. The only thing that gave Kristen hope that Dani hadn't actually murdered the three guys was the gray car that had followed her on multiple occasions. Dani and another deputy had chased the car out of town after it had evaded a routine stop. Her mind kept coming back to Steve. He'd been the leader of the group when they'd attacked her. Dani said he'd strayed away from the other guys. He could've easily snuck back into town, killing each guy and making it look like she did it, but how did he know she was back? Maybe he'd followed her.

It was possible he knew everything about her life, where she lived, where she worked, and who she hung around. Kristen shivered with fear at the thought of Steve Olsen following her around. She decided to drive over to Dani's parents' store and hang out until Dani got off her shift. She barely knew anyone in town anymore and wasn't sure who she could trust, but she didn't want to be alone. The thought of Dani and her family made Kristen feel safe.

She backed out of her driveway and headed down Lake Drive, turning onto the main road leading away from the lake. She was only a few blocks from her house when she noticed the car in her rearview mirror, riding very close to her.

"Oh God," she said, terrified, as she shakily tried to scroll through her phone.

*

Dani was an hour from the end of her day. The twelve-hour shifts were starting to take a toll on her and she'd barely slept in the last three days. She yawned, rummaging through the junk food everyone kept in the break room.

"Don't throw anything out," Sheriff Fisher called from behind her.

"Who said I was throwing anything away?" she asked, spinning around to face him with the last package of cookies in her hand.

He raised an eyebrow. "I seriously doubt you're going to eat those. Give them here."

She yawned again. "I'm tired, I'm hungry, and I'm eating these whether you like it or not." She grinned, opening the package.

"I knew you'd give up that health crap and come over to the dark side," he said, snapping a picture of her with his phone. "Evidence," he added.

"Oh, for crying out loud." She shook her head at him. Her phone rang in her pocket before she could eat the cookie she was holding. She noticed Kristen's name on the caller ID.

"Hey," Dani answered. "I was just thinking about you. Do you want to get dinner—"

"Where are you?" Kristen shrieked.

"The sheriff's office. Why? What's wrong?"

Kristen didn't say anything.

"Kristen? Are you there?" Dani's chest tightened. Sheriff Fisher raised an eyebrow.

"Dani! Help!"

"Kristen! Where are you? What's wrong?"

"The car ... following me ... Ced—"

Dani heard tires squealing as the line went dead. "That car's chasing Kristen. I think she's on Cedar!" she yelled to him as she ran out of the building, trying to call Kristen again when she reached her SUV.

Sheriff Fisher radioed dispatch to send all units to Cedar Street along with EMTs as he jumped into his cruiser and raced out of the parking lot with his siren wailing and lights flashing behind Dani.

"Fuck!" Dani yelled, trying over and over, but Kristen's phone kept going directly to voicemail.

"Sheriff, her phone's dead," she radioed.

"Copy. All available units have been dispatched to respond to a possible car chase or accident on Cedar."

"Roger."

"Dispatch, this is Deputy Nyman. Be advised, I'm on scene of an MVA with injuries in the fourteen hundred block of Cedar Street. Copy?"

"Copy, EMTs are two minutes out."

Dani keyed her microphone. "Nyman, is it a blue sedan?"

"Yes, ma'am. It's upside down in the ditch. The driver is unconscious and there are no passengers. Copy?"

"Roger." Dani fought back the tears, silently praying to God Kristen was okay. "Do you see any other vehicles?"

"Negative."

"Dispatch, Chief Ricketts. Put out an emergency BOLO for a gray two-door Nissan with a white male driver. It may appear to have been in an accident and is more than likely headed out of town. Copy?'

"Roger, Chief."

Dani saw the flashing red and white lights of the ambulance and blue lights of the sheriff's office cruiser as she turned the corner. She floored the gas and skidded to a stop on the side of the road and threw the SUV into park. She'd barely got the engine cut off when she jumped out and ran around the ambulance. Kristen's car was sitting on its roof down in the ditch, off the side of the road near the woods. All the glass was busted out and the sides were smashed in, indicating that the car had rolled a few times before coming to a stop. She ran up to the passenger side window where the EMTs and firefighters were pulling Kristen out of the mangled car.

"Is she—"

"She's breathing, but she's unconscious," one of the men said as they rushed the stretcher towards the ambulance.

"Ricketts," Sheriff Fisher yelled.

Dani looked up to see him waving his hand for her to come over to him. Dani grabbed Kristen's hand. "I'm here, Kristen. It's Dani. You're going to be okay … I love you," she whispered to her as they put her in the back of the waiting vehicle. She watched them close the doors and drive away with the only person she'd ever loved.

"There are aggressive tire tracks over here and I have a good feeling we're going to see gray paint on the other side of her car. It looks like she was run off the road."

"Whoever did this was trying to kill her. I knew it!"

"What? What do you know?" he asked.

"Whoever is driving that car is not only our killer; he's also been after her for weeks. I think she's supposed to be next," Dani said. She wanted to tell him everything, but she didn't trust Mayor Olsen. She wasn't sure what he'd do if he knew it was his son doing all of this.

"We have to find that fucking car!" he shouted to the other deputies that had arrived at the scene.

"From the looks of her car, I'd say his is probably damaged too. He could be broken down nearby or on the outskirts of town," Dani added. She wanted to search the city for his last address, but without a warrant or probable cause there wasn't much she could do. "I'm heading over to the hospital. Call me if you get anything."

*

Dani skidded to a stop outside the emergency entrance to the local hospital. Henry was walking down the hall when she walked through the double doors.

"What brings you in here?" he asked.

"MVA," she replied, hurrying down the hall.

175

The small hospital was only three stories high with a small emergency department, maternity ward and regular doctor's offices on the first floor, along with the morgue. The second floor was used for intensive care and surgeries and the top floor was all regular inpatient care rooms.

"May I help you, Chief?" The woman at the desk asked.

"A woman was brought in from an MVA about twenty minutes ago."

"Yes, I'll show you to her," she said, walking around the desk and leading Dani behind one of the curtains separating the emergency room beds.

Kristen was lying on a gurney with a cervical collar around her neck, an IV line in her arm, and a blood pressure cuff on her upper arm. One of the doctors was standing next to her, writing on a clipboard.

"Has she woken up?"

"Yes. She woke up on arrival," he replied. "Nothing's broken and all her scans look good. She has a concussion and mild bruising from the seatbelt. She'll be sore for the next few days. I just gave her some pain medication, so she's sleeping at the moment."

"Thank God," Dani whispered, grabbing her pale hand as she sat down in the chair next to the gurney. When he left the room, she bowed her head, kissing the back of Kristen's warm hand before pressing her forehead against it. "I love you so much. I don't think I could bear losing you again," she murmured.

Kristen's vision was slightly blurry as she opened her eyes. The throbbing pain in her head felt like a bass drum. The fuzziness in the room finally cleared enough for her to see Dani slumped over near her side. She moved the hand

Dani was holding, encouraging her to lift her head so she could see the eyes that melted her heart.

Dani turned her head up to see watery chocolate brown eyes looking back at her. She quickly moved up to Kristen's head, kissing her cheek softly and brushing the bangs off her forehead.

"You scared the hell out of me," she whispered.

"All I remember is seeing that gray car."

"I was at the station talking to Sheriff Fisher when you called to tell me he was following you. That's when he ran you off the road. You went for a pretty wild ride, but the doctor said nothing's broken. You have a lot of bruising and a concussion, so you're going to be in a lot of pain tomorrow."

"I feel like someone slapped me across the face with a bag of bricks."

Dani grinned. "You don't look like it though."

"Ever the flirt," Kristen chided softly.

"How is your head feeling?" the doctor asked, walking back into the room.

"It's throbbing."

"That's to be expected." He flashed a penlight into her eyes. "How's your vision."

"It's not fuzzy anymore."

"Good. I just took another look at your CT scan. I'd like to keep you overnight for observation."

Kristen nodded and watched him walk out of the room.

"I'm going to go call the sheriff. I'll be back in a few minutes," Dani said as she leaned over, kissing Kristen's cheek.

Dani walked out into the hall with mixed emotion. She was glad Kristen was going to be okay, but she was seething with anger deep inside for the bastard that had tried to take her life.

Chapter 22

The next morning, Kristen was sitting on the edge of the bed. The cervical collar was gone, as well as the IV line and other attachments. She was slightly lost in thought when she heard footsteps coming down the hall, bringing her attention back to the room. She smiled casually when Dani appeared in the doorway. Despite all the confusion and lies that had come between them recently, Kristen still felt the familiar tightening in her chest and tug of arousal low in her belly when she saw Dani. If there ever was such a thing as soul mates, she knew without a doubt that Dani Ricketts was hers.

"You look better." Dani grinned, noticing the color had returned to her face.

"I still feel like I was hit by a truck, but I'm ready to get the hell out of here," she said, hopping down off the bed and crossing the room.

"Did you talk to your parents?" Dani asked, wrapping her arms around her.

"Yeah. They insisted on coming to get me, but I assured them that I'm okay. I didn't tell them anything, except that I was in a small car accident." Kristen returned the hug and pulled away.

Dani nodded, pursing her lips in thought as they walked down the hallway. "Do you want to go to your house, or would you be more comfortable at my place?"

"My house is fine."

*

"Are you sure you don't want me to stay?" Dani asked, threading her arms around Kristen's waist. They were standing in the kitchen of her house.

"No. Go back to work and stop worrying about me." Kristen put her hand on Dani's cheek and smiled. "I'll be fine. I have calls to make to the insurance company and the salvage yard that has my car. Plus, I need to call my parents again."

"You need to rest and probably eat something. It's almost lunchtime."

Kristen laughed softly and kissed her lips. "I'm not going to want to sleep if you hang around and you know it," she said, raising an eyebrow suggestively.

Dani grinned. "Okay, I'll be back when my shift ends. Call me if you need anything," she said, unable to argue with the beautiful woman in her arms. She wasn't sure she'd be able to let her sleep anyway.

Kristen walked her to the door. Dani kissed her gently, lingering for a slightly deeper kiss before Kristen pushed her out the door with a smile on her face.

*

Dani walked into Sheriff Fisher's office, peeling the banana in her hand.

"How's she doing?" he asked when she sat down.

"She has a pretty bad headache, but other than that just has sore muscles from the accident."

"She's lucky to be alive," he muttered, shaking his head.

"I take it no one's seen the car," Dani said, taking a generous bite of the fruit.

"Nope. He could be long gone."

"I stopped to see the car on my way in. He definitely hit her a few times. The driver's side has gray paint down the side of it, so his car should be damaged. The problem with that is, he may switch cars and then we'll really be screwed."

"I talked to the mayor this morning about roadblocks, but he made a good point. We have no idea what this guy looks like or even what his name is."

Dani bit the inside of her mouth. She trusted the sheriff, but she wasn't sure if the mayor knew the truth about his son or even how far he'd go to protect him. That was the reason Kristen's family hadn't trusted the legal system in the first place. Steve Olsen's father had been the sheriff and he'd had the mayor at the time in his back pocket.

"Take a ride with me," she said.

Sheriff Fisher furrowed his brow.

Dani nodded towards the door for him to follow her. When they stepped outside, she walked into the middle of the parking lot.

"I know who it is."

"What do you mean?" he asked.

"It's a long story that actually goes back to my senior year of high school, but the mayor's son, Steve Olsen, is behind the murders and he's also the person that tried to kill Kristen yesterday."

"What? That's a huge accusation, Dani."

"I found out recently that the three dead guys and Steve gang raped Kristen at the end of our senior year. That's why her family moved away so abruptly. Olsen's father was the sheriff at the time, and they didn't trust him."

"Oh my God. Why are you just now finding this out?"

"Steve has been trying to frame her, and she was scared. I don't blame her. If Mayor Olsen gets wind of this, he'll throw the book at her, evidence or not, that's a pretty strong motive."

"Why did she come back?"

"To sell the house and move on with her life," Dani sighed. "I know she didn't kill those guys."

"Well, if there's no evidence, a motive alone isn't enough to prosecute anyone."

"I wouldn't be so sure. This can't come out. Mayor Olsen will do anything to protect his son, including dragging her through the mud and she's a victim herself. Olsen let his kid get away with a lot when he was sheriff."

"Yeah, but rape?"

Dani shrugged. "Her parents didn't want to take a chance at having their daughter destroyed any further. Hell, I wouldn't either. In my opinion, those bastards got what they deserved."

"Why do you think Steve came back in the first place?"

"I think one of the guys got wind that she was back in town, and they got scared, maybe they thought she was going to finally turn them in."

"The statute of limitations has passed."

"They don't know that. We're talking about three lowlife drug users."

Sheriff Fisher nodded his head in agreement. "If they were all friends, they probably kept in touch. That's probably how Steve found out."

"Exactly. Who knows, maybe they were going to turn themselves in or something stupid. Either way, Steve killed them all and now he's after her."

"What a cluster fuck!" he yelled.

Kristen closed her eyes to rest her head not long after Dani left and fell asleep on the couch. She was dreaming about Dani when something grabbed her. She jerked in her sleep, opening her eyes. She realized someone was holding her down. She fought to get free and tried to scream, but suddenly, she felt a sharp pain in her head and everything went black.

Kristen came to a few minutes later. Her head throbbed like a bass drum, and her vision was fuzzy and doubled. She could barely make out the person sitting across from her. She tried to move, but she was tied to one of her dining room chairs.

The man waited, watching her get her bearings as the fog in her head cleared. Her eyes finally landed on him.

"Did you miss me?" he sneered.

Kristen froze when she realized it was Steve Olsen looking back at her.

"I knew you were going to be a problem. I wanted to kill you twelve years ago, but no, Roger, Paul, and Larry were a bunch of pussies. They only wanted to fuck the little dyke bitch and toss you away because they were scared of my dad," he growled, shaking his head. His clothes were dirty, and his face was scruffy. He looked like he hadn't showered in days.

"Steve … I never told—"

"Close your mouth, whore!" he shouted.

She grimaced. His words felt like a slap across her face. "Why did you kill Roger, Paul, and Larry?"

He lunged at her, squeezing her upper arms and shaking her violently. "I didn't kill anyone! You killed my friends and thought you could get me too, but I'm smart!

183

I'm going to sit here and watch you die slowly and then piss on your dead body!" he screamed.

"Steve, I didn't kill them."

"You fucking lying bitch!" he shouted, pulling a gun from his pocket and pointing it at her head. "You're going to call your cop girlfriend and tell her everything," he said, grabbing her phone from the counter and scrolling for Dani's number. "You tell her to come here and nothing else or I'll put a hole in your head." He held the gun to her forehead with one hand and the phone to her ear with the other.

Tears ran down her cheeks as she listened to the phone ring.

Chapter 23

Dani walked back inside the building. Sheriff Fisher had returned to his desk, trying to figure out a way to catch Steve Olsen without alerting the mayor.

"Hey, I just got a weird call from Kristen. I don't think she's feeling well."

"Take the rest of the day off. I'd feel better knowing you were with her anyway," he said.

"Yeah, I was thinking the same thing. I hated leaving her alone this morning, but she's stubborn and she insisted. I'll check in with you later," she replied, leaving the room.

Kristen sounded upset, like she'd been crying, when she called and asked Dani to come over as soon as possible. Dani pulled out of the parking lot of the sheriff's office and drove towards Lake Drive, going much faster than the speed limit because she didn't like the feeling in the pit of her stomach.

*

Kristen was sitting in the dining room, tied to the chair with a piece of duct tape over her mouth when she heard Dani pull into the driveway. She tried to make noise, but there was nothing she could do.

Dani knocked on the door and it swung open, but no one was there. She stepped inside, looking around the living room. Suddenly, she was tackled from behind. Her instincts kicked in and she grappled with the person on her back, but he was twice her size and finally wrestled her gun away from her.

"Sit down you dyke bitch!" he yelled, pointing the gun at her head.

Dani barely recognized Steve Olsen. He looked much older than thirty. She looked around for Kristen, hoping she wasn't too late, and finally saw her in the dining room. She moved back towards Kristen, sitting in the chair next to her.

He walked over, snatching the tape from Kristen's mouth. "Tell her!" he shouted. "Tell your whore what you did!"

"Steve, I didn't kill them," Kristen said.

He pointed the gun at Dani's head. "I'm going to kill her first, and then you so it looks like you did it before shooting yourself you guilty bitch! Everyone will know the truth. They'll know what you did."

"I didn't kill anyone, Steve," she said as tears rolled down her cheeks. "Please don't hurt her," she whispered.

"Stop lying!" he yelled, pointing the gun back towards Kristen. "You're dead you fucking bitch! Dead!" he screamed.

"I did it, you mother fucker!" Dani shouted as a loud bang echoed in the room. Steve's limp body collapsed in front of Kristen.

She looked down at the hole above his right eye and the crimson blood pooling under his head, before turning her eyes to Dani, who was sitting next to her with a blank stare on her face and a small black revolver in her hand.

"Dani?" she said softly.

Dani finally looked over at her. "I'm sorry," she muttered. "I couldn't let them hurt you again."

"No, never be sorry for protecting me." Kristen wished she could get out of the bindings holding her to the chair as she struggled to free herself.

"Wait a second." Dani tucked the gun away in the ankle holster on her leg and untied her.

Kristen flew into her arms. She'd never felt safer in all her life than at that moment. "I love you so much," she said, kissing her with everything she had.

Dani kissed her back and pulled away. "You don't hate me?"

"No! Why would you say that? I'm shocked, but I could never hate you."

Dani nodded towards the dead body. "I'm a murderer," she sighed, turning her eyes back to Kristen.

"All you did was protect me."

"I—"

"Those bastards hurt me once and he was trying to kill me. They got what they deserved. I just wish you would've said something to me, but I understand now. If you'd told me it was you, I may have tried to stop you, and this needed to be done. As far as I'm concerned, you gave me my life back, Dani." Kristen moved back into her arms. "I love you."

Dani was slightly shocked to see Kristen's reaction. "I love you too, but what are we going to do about the dead man on the floor?" Dani shook her head. "I need to tell the sheriff about all of this."

"Steve killed the other guys and came after me, and you saved me. That's what happened here and that's what you're going to tell him," Kristen exclaimed, looking at her sternly. "I lost you once because of these assholes and I'm not about to do it again."

Dani raised her eyebrows and shrugged. "I better call this in."

Epilogue

Kristen was lying on her back in a red bikini, shielding her eyes from the hot sun beating down above her.

"Have you made your decision?" she asked, looking at the woman next to her. Dani was sitting at the end of the dock with her feet swinging back and forth above the water, holding a fishing pole.

"I don't know," she sighed, looking back at her through the dark lenses of her sunglasses. "With everything that happened a few months ago, do you really think I should be running for anything?"

"Yes, and so does the rest of this town."

Dani shrugged. "But mayor?"

"Why not? You said it yourself, Joe Fisher is a good sheriff, and you trust him. There's no need to replace him. Besides, think about what you can do for this community as the mayor. You can keep everyone safe and stop the influx of city folk that are trying to ruin the laidback, lake house lifestyle that you love so much, at the same time. Since Olsen announced his retirement, no one has come forward saying they're running, because everyone is waiting for you to step up to the plate."

"What about you?" Dani asked.

"What about me? If I'm not mistaken you moved into my house, so the entire town knows about us." She ran her hand over Dani's thigh. "I'm not going anywhere anytime soon. Unless it's inside to get naked with you," Kristen teased.

Dani chuckled, pushing her hand away. "You look sinful enough as it is. I don't think those couple of pieces of cloth you're wearing can be called a bathing suit."

"You like it don't you?" she whispered seductively.

"Yes, of course. I'm not dead, and neither is Mr. Cranston for that matter," Dani replied, waving to the old man who was sitting on his dock, looking their way.

"Oh, good God." Kristen shook her head, following her line of sight. "Poor bastard," she giggled.

Dani laughed as the pole in her hands shook. She snatched it back, reeling hard. Kristen watched as she fought the pole. The end of Dani's line reached the dock, and she flung it towards Kristen.

"Dani!" Kristen shrieked, fumbling with what she thought was a fish in her lap. She looked down to see a small plastic vile with a scroll inside of it. She opened the end, pulling the paper out and squinted in the sun to read it. *I'll be the mayor, if you'll be my wife.* "Wow. I … are you sure?"

"I won't do it unless you're beside me." Dani smiled.

"I guess we're turning in the mayoral paperwork and applying for a marriage license in the morning," Kristen squealed and climbed into her lap, kissing her passionately.

Dani kissed her back, running her hands over the nearly naked body in her arms. "If you're trying to kill Mr. Cranston, I know a lot better ways than a heart attack," she whispered playfully in her ear.

"Oh, I'm sure you do," Kristen laughed, rolling her eyes.

About the Author

Graysen Morgen is the bestselling author of *Falling Snow*, *Fast Pitch*, and *Bridesmaid of Honor*, as well as many other titles. She was born and raised in North Florida with winding rivers and waterways at her back door and the white sandy beach a mile away. She has spent most of her lifetime in the sun and on the water. She enjoys reading, writing, fishing, and spending as much time as possible with her wife and their children.

You can contact Graysen at graysenmorgen@aol.com and follow her on Instagram @graysenmorgen and on Facebook.com/graysenmorgen

Other Titles Available From Triplicity Publishing

Crashing Waves by Graysen Morgen. After a tragic accident, Pro Surfer, Rory Eden, spends her days hiding in the surf and snowboard manufacturing company that she built from the ground up, while living her life as a shell of the person that she once was. Rory's world is turned upside when a young surfer pursues her, asking for the one thing she can't do. Adler Troy and Dr. Cason Macauley from Graysen Morgen's best seller, *Falling Snow,* make an appearance in this romantic adventure about life, love, and letting go.

Bridesmaid of Honor by Graysen Morgen. Britton Prescott's best friend is getting married and she's the maid of honor. As if that isn't enough to deal with, Britton's sister announces she's getting married in the same month and her maid of honor is her best friend Daphne, the same woman who has tormented Britton for years. Britton has to suck it up and play nice, instead of scratching her eyes out, because she and Daphne are in both weddings. Everyone is counting on them to behave like adults.

Falling Snow by Graysen Morgen. Dr. Cason Macauley, a high-speed trauma surgeon from Denver meets Adler Troy, a professional snowboarder and sparks fly. The last thing Cason wants is a relationship and Adler doesn't realize what's right in front of her until it's gone, but will it be too late?

Fate vs. Destiny by Graysen Morgen. Logan Greer devotes her life to investigating plane crashes for the National Transportation Safety Board. Brooke McCabe is an investigator with the Federal Aviation Association who literally flies by the seat of her pants. When Logan gets tangled in head games with both women will she choose fate or destiny?

Just Me by Graysen Morgen. Wild child Ian Wiley has to grow up and take the reins of the hundred year old family business when tragedy strikes. Cassidy Harland is a little surprised that she came within an inch of picking up a gorgeous stranger in a bar and is shocked to find out that stranger is the new head of her company.

Love Loss Revenge by Graysen Morgen. Rian Casey is an FBI Agent working the biggest case of her career and madly in love with her girlfriend. Her world is turned upside when tragedy strikes. Heartbroken, she tries to rebuild her life. When she discovers the truth behind what really happened that awful night she decides justice isn't good enough, and vows revenge on everyone involved.

Natural Instinct by Graysen Morgen. Chandler Scott is a Marine Biologist who keeps her private life private. Corey Joslen is intrigued by Chandler from the moment she meets her. Chandler is forced to finally open her life up to Corey. It backfires in Corey's face and sends her running. Will either woman learn to trust her natural instinct?

Secluded Heart by Graysen Morgen. Chase Leery is an overworked cardiac surgeon with a group of best friends that have an opinion and a reason for everything. When she meets a new artist named Remy Sheridan at her best friend's art gallery she is captivated by the reclusive woman. When Chase finds out why Remy is so sheltered will she put her career on the line to help her or is it too difficult to love someone with a secluded heart?

In Love, at War by Graysen Morgen. Charley Hayes is in the Army Air Force and stationed at Ford Island in Pearl Harbor. She is the commanding officer of her own female-only service squadron and doing the one thing she loves most, repairing airplanes. Life is good for Charley, until the day she finds herself falling in love while fighting for her life as her country is thrown haphazardly into World War II. Can she survive being in love and at war?

Fast Pitch by Graysen Morgen. Graham Cahill is a senior in college and the catcher and captain of the softball team. Despite being an all-star pitcher, Bailey Michaels is young and arrogant. Graham and Bailey are forced to get to know each other off the field in order to learn to work together on the field. Will the extra time pay off or will it drive a nail through the team?

Submerged by Graysen Morgen. Assistant District Attorney Layne Carmichael had no idea that the sexy woman she took home from a local bar for a one night stand would turn out to be someone she would be prosecuting months later. Scooter is a Naval Officer on a submarine who changes women like she changes uniforms. When she is accused of a heinous crime she is shocked to see her latest conquest sitting across from her as the prosecuting attorney.

Vow of Solitude by Austen Thorne. Detective Jordan Denali is in a fight for her life against the ghosts from her past and a Serial Killer taunting her with his every move. She lives a life of solitude and plans to keep it that way. When Callie Marceau, a curious Medical Examiner, decides she wants in on the biggest case of her career, as well as, Jordan's life, Jordan is powerless to stop her.

Igniting Temptation by Sydney Canyon. Mackenzie Trotter is the Head of Pediatrics at the local hospital. Her life takes a rather unexpected turn when she meets a flirtatious, beautiful fire fighter. Both women soon discover it doesn't take much to ignite temptation.

One Night by Sydney Canyon. While on a business trip, Caylen Jarrett spends an amazing night with a beautiful stripper. Months later, she is shocked and confused when that same woman re-enters her life. The fact that this stranger could destroy her career doesn't bother her. C.J. is more terrified of the feelings this woman stirs in her. Could she have fallen in love in one night and not even known it?

Fine by Sydney Canyon. Collin Anderson hides behind a façade, pretending everything is fine. Her workaholic wife and best friend are both oblivious as she goes on an emotional journey, battling a potentially hereditary disease that her mother has been diagnosed with. The only person who knows what is really going on, is Collin's doctor. The same doctor, who is an acquaintance that she's always been attracted to, and who has a partner of her own.

Shadow's Eyes by Sydney Canyon. Tyler McCain is the owner of a large ranch that breeds and sells different types of horses. She isn't exactly thrilled when a Hollywood movie producer shows up wanting to film his latest movie on her property.

Reegan Delsol is an up and coming actress who has everything going for her when she lands the lead role in a new film, but there one small problem that could blow the entire picture.